THE VULTURES OF WHAPETON

BY

ROBERT E. HOWARD

British Library Cataloguing-in-Publication Data
A catalogue record for this book is available from the
British Library

Contents

Robert E. Howard

Robert Ervin Howard was born in Peaster, Texas in 1906. During his youth, his family moved between a variety of Texan boomtowns, and Howard – a bookish and somewhat introverted child – was steeped in the violent myths and legends of the Old South. Although he loved reading and learning, Howard developed a distinctly Texan, hardboiled outlook on the world. He became a passionate fan of boxing, taking it up at an amateur level, and from the age of nine began to write adventure tales of semi-historical bloodshed. In 1919, when Howard was thirteen, his family moved to the Central Texas hamlet of Cross Plains, where he would stay for the rest of his life.

At fifteen Howard began to read the pulp magazines of the day, and to write more seriously. The December 1922 issue of his high school newspaper featured two of his stories, 'Golden Hope Christmas' and 'West is West'. In 1924 he sold his first piece – a short caveman tale titled 'Spear and Fang' – for $16 to the not-yet-famous *Weird Tales* magazine. He published with the magazine regularly over the next few years. 1929 was a breakout year for Howard, in that the 23-year-old writer began to sell to other magazines, such as *Ghost Stories* and *Argosy*, both of whom had previously sent him hundreds of rejection slips. In 1930, he began a correspondence with weird fiction master H. P. Lovecraft which ran up to his death six years later, and is regarded as one of the great correspondence cycles in all of fantasy literature.

It was partly due to Lovecraft's encouragement that Howard created his most famous character, Conan the Cimmerian. Conan – a barbarian-turned-King during the Hyborian Age, a mythical period of some 12,000 years ago – featured in seventeen *Weird Tales* stories between 1933 and 1936, and is now regarded as having spawned the 'sword and sorcery' genre, making Howard's influence on fantasy literature comparable to that of J. R. R. Tolkien's. The Conan stories have since been adapted many times, most famously in the series of films starring Arnold Schwarzenegger.

Howard was enjoying an all-time high in sales by the beginning of 1936, but he was also deeply upset by the ill health of his mother, who had fallen into a coma. On the morning of June 11, 1936, he asked an attending nurse whether she would ever recover, and the nurse replied negatively. Howard walked to his car, parked outside the family home in Cross Plains, and shot himself. He died eight hours later, aged just thirty.

CHAPTER 1 GUNS IN THE DARK

The bare plank walls of the Golden Eagle Saloon seemed still to vibrate with the crashing echoes of the guns which had split the sudden darkness with spurts of red. But only a nervous shuffling of booted feet sounded in the tense silence that followed the shots. Then somewhere a match rasped on leather and a yellow flicker sprang up, etching a shaky hand and a pallid face. An instant later an oil lamp with a broken chimney illuminated the saloon, throwing tense bearded faces into bold relief. The big lamp that hung from the ceiling was a smashed ruin; kerosene dripped from it to the floor, making an oily puddle beside a grimmer, darker pool.

Two figures held the center of the room, under the broken lamp. One lay facedown, motionless arms outstretching empty hands. The other was crawling to his feet, blinking and gaping stupidly, like a man whose wits are still muddled by drink. His right arm hung limply by his side, a long-barreled pistol sagging from his fingers.

The rigid line of figures along the bar melted into movement. Men came forward, stooping to stare down at the limp shape. A confused babble of conversation rose. Hurried steps sounded outside, and the crowd divided as a man pushed his way abruptly through. Instantly he dominated the scene. His broad-shouldered, trim-hipped figure was above medium height, and his broad-brimmed white hat, neat boots and cravat contrasted with the rough garb of the others, just as his keen, dark face with its narrow black mustache contrasted with the bearded countenances about him. He held an ivory-butted gun in his right hand, muzzle tilted upward.

"What devil's work is this?" he harshly demanded; and then his gaze fell on the man on the floor. His eyes widened.

"Grimes!" he ejaculated. "Jim Grimes, my deputy! Who did this?" There was something tigerish about him as he wheeled toward the uneasy crowd. "Who did this?" he demanded, half-crouching, his gun still lifted, but seeming to hover like a live thing ready to swoop.

Feet shuffled as men backed away, but one man spoke up: "We don't know, Middleton. Jackson there was havin' a little fun, shootin' at the ceilin', and the rest of us was at the bar, watchin' him, when Grimes come in and started to arrest him--"

"So Jackson shot him!" snarled Middleton, his gun covering the befuddled one in a baffling blur of motion. Jackson yelped in fear and threw up his hands, and the man who had first spoken interposed.

"No, Sheriff, it couldn't have been Jackson. His gun was empty when the lights went out. I know he slung six bullets into the ceilin' while he was playin' the fool, and I heard him snap the gun three times afterwards, so I know it was empty. But when Grimes went up to him, somebody shot the light out, and a gun banged in the dark, and when we got a light on again, there Grimes was on the floor, and Jackson was just gettin' up."

"I didn't shoot him," muttered Jackson. "I was just havin' a little fun. I was drunk, but I ain't now. I wouldn't have resisted arrest. When the light went out I didn't know what had happened. I heard the gun bang, and Grimes dragged me down with him as he fell. I didn't shoot him. I dunno who did."

"None of us knows," added a bearded miner. "Somebody shot in the dark--"

"More'n one," muttered another. "I heard at least three or four guns speakin'."

Silence followed, in which each man looked sidewise at his neighbor. The men had drawn back to the bar, leaving the middle of the big room clear, where the sheriff stood. Suspicion and fear galvanized the crowd, leaping like an electric spark from man to man. Each man knew that a murderer stood near him, possibly at his elbow. Men refused to look directly into the eyes of their neighbors, fearing to surprise guilty knowledge there--and die for the discovery. They stared at the sheriff who stood facing them, as if expecting to see him fall suddenly before a blast from the same unknown guns that had mowed down his deputy.

Middleton's steely eyes ranged along the silent line of men. Their eyes avoided or gave back his stare. In some he read fear; some were inscrutable; in others flickered a sinister mockery.

"The men who killed Jim Grimes are in this saloon," he said finally. "Some of you are the murderers." He was careful not to let his eyes single out anyone when he spoke; they swept the whole assemblage.

"I've been expecting this. Things have been getting a little too hot for the robbers and murderers who have been terrorizing this camp, so they've started shooting my deputies in the back. I suppose you'll try to kill me, next. Well, I want to tell you sneaking rats, whoever you are, that I'm ready for you, any time."

He fell silent, his rangy frame tense, his eyes burning with watchful alertness. None moved. The men along the bar might have been figures cut from stone.

He relaxed and shoved his gun into its scabbard; a sneer twisted his lips.

"I know your breed. You won't shoot a man unless his back is toward you. Forty men have been murdered in the vicinity of this camp within the last year, and not one had a chance to defend himself.

"Maybe this killing is an ultimatum to me. All right; I've got an answer ready: I've got a new deputy, and you won't find him so easy as Grimes. I'm fighting fire with fire from here on. I'm riding out of the Gulch early in the morning, and when I come back, I'll have a man with me. A gunfighter from Texas!"

He paused to let this information sink in, and laughed grimly at the furtive glances that darted from man to man.

"You'll find him no lamb," he predicted vindictively. "He was too wild for the country where gun-throwing was invented. What he did down there is none of my business. What he'll do here is what counts. And all I ask is that the men who murdered Grimes here, try that same trick on this Texan.

"Another thing, on my own account. I'm meeting this man at Ogalala Spring tomorrow morning. I'll be riding out alone, at dawn. If anybody wants to try to waylay me, let him make his plans now! I'll follow the open trail, and anyone who has any business with me will find me ready."

And turning his trimly-tailored back scornfully on the throng at the bar, the sheriff of Whapeton strode from the saloon.

* * *

Ten miles east of Whapeton a man squatted on his heels, frying strips of deer meat over a tiny fire. The sun was just coming up. A short distance away a rangy mustang nibbled

7

at the wiry grass that grew sparsely between broken rocks. The man had camped there that night, but his saddle and blanket were hidden back in the bushes. That fact showed him to be a man of wary nature. No one following the trail that led past Ogalala Spring could have seen him as he slept among the bushes. Now, in full daylight, he was making no attempt to conceal his presence.

The man was tall, broad-shouldered, deep-chested, lean-hipped, like one who had spent his life in the saddle. His unruly black hair matched a face burned dark by the sun, but his eyes were a burning blue. Low on either hip the black butt of a heavy Colt jutted from a worn black leather scabbard. These guns seemed as much part of the man as his eyes or his hands. He had worn them so constantly and so long that their association was as natural as the use of his limbs.

As he fried his meat and watched his coffee boiling in a battered old pot, his gaze darted continually eastward where the trail crossed a wide open space before it vanished among the thickets of a broken hill country. Westward the trail mounted a gentle slope and quickly disappeared among trees and bushes that crowded up within a few yards of the spring. But it was always eastward that the man looked.

When a rider emerged from the thickets to the east, the man at the spring set aside the skillet with its sizzling meat strips, and picked up his rifle--a long range Sharps .50.

His eyes narrowed with satisfaction. He did not rise, but remained on one knee, the rifle resting negligently in his hands, the muzzle tilted upward, not aimed.

The rider came straight on, and the man at the spring watched him from under the brim of his hat. Only when the stranger pulled up a few yards away did the first man lift his head and give the other a full view of his face.

The horseman was a supple youth of medium height, and his hat did not conceal the fact that his hair was yellow and curly. His wide eyes were ingenuous, and an infectious smile curved his lips. There was no rifle under his knee, but an ivory-butted .45 hung low at his right hip.

His expression as he saw the other man's face gave no hint to his reaction, except for a slight, momentary contraction of the muscles that control the eyes--a movement involuntary and all but uncontrollable. Then he grinned broadly, and hailed:

"That meat smells prime, stranger!"

"Light and help me with it," invited the other instantly. "Coffee, too, if you don't mind drinkin' out of the pot."

He laid aside the rifle as the other swung from his saddle. The blond youngster threw his reins over the horse's head, fumbled in his blanket roll and drew out a battered tin cup. Holding this in his right hand he approached the fire with the rolling gait of a man born to a horse.

"I ain't et my breakfast," he admitted. "Camped down the trail a piece last night, and come on up here early to meet a man. Thought you was the *hombre* till you looked up. Kinda startled me," he added frankly. He sat down opposite the taller man, who shoved the skillet and coffee pot toward him. The tall man moved both these utensils with his left hand. His right rested lightly and apparently casually on his right thigh.

The youth filled his tin cup, drank the black, unsweetened coffee with evident enjoyment, and filled the cup again. He picked out pieces of the cooling meat with his fingers--and he was careful to use only his left hand for that part of the breakfast that would leave grease on his fingers. But he used his right hand for pouring coffee and holding the cup to his lips. He did not seem to notice the position of the other's right hand.

"Name's Glanton," he confided. "Billy Glanton. Texas. Guadalupe country. Went up the trail with a herd of mossy horns, went broke buckin' faro in Hayes City, and headed west lookin' for gold. Hell of a prospector I turned out to be! Now I'm lookin' for a job, and the man I was goin' to meet here said he had one for me. If I read your marks right you're a Texan, too?"

The last sentence was more a statement than a question.

"That's my brand," grunted the other. "Name's O'Donnell. Pecos River country, originally."

His statement, like that of Glanton's, was indefinite. Both the Pecos and the Guadalupe cover considerable areas of territory. But Glanton grinned boyishly and stuck out his hand.

"Shake!" he cried. "I'm glad to meet an *hombre* from my home state, even if our stampin' grounds down there are a right smart piece apart!"

Their hands met and locked briefly--brown, sinewy hands that had never worn gloves, and that gripped with the abrupt tension of steel springs.

The handshake seemed to relax O'Donnell. When he poured out another cup of coffee he held the cup in one hand and the pot in the other, instead of setting the cup on the ground beside him and pouring with his left hand.

"I've been in California," he volunteered. "Drifted back on this side of the mountains a month ago. Been in Whapeton for the last few weeks, but gold huntin' ain't my style. I'm a *vaquero*. Never should have tried to be anything else. I'm headin' back for Texas."

"Why don't you try Kansas?" asked Glanton. "It's fillin' up with Texas men, bringin' cattle up the trail to stock the ranges. Within a year they'll be drivin' 'em into Wyoming and Montana."

11

"Maybe I might." O'Donnell lifted the coffee cup absently. He held it in his left hand, and his right lay in his lap, almost touching the big black pistol butt. But the tension was gone out of his frame. He seemed relaxed, absorbed in what Glanton was saying. The use of his left hand and the position of his right seemed mechanical, merely an unconscious habit.

"It's a great country," declared Glanton, lowering his head to conceal the momentary and uncontrollable flicker of triumph in his eyes. "Fine ranges. Towns springin' up wherever the railroad touches.

"Everybody gettin' rich on Texas beef. Talkin' about 'cattle kings'! Wish I could have knowed this beef boom was comin' when I was a kid! I'd have rounded up about fifty thousand of them maverick steers that was roamin' loose all over lower Texas, and put me a brand on 'em, and saved 'em for the market!" He laughed at his own conceit.

"They wasn't worth six bits a head then," he added, as men in making small talk will state a fact well known to everyone. "Now twenty dollars a head ain't the top price."

He emptied his cup and set it on the ground near his right hip. His easy flow of speech flowed on--but the natural movement of his hand away from the cup turned into a blur of speed that flicked the heavy gun from its scabbard.

Two shots roared like one long stuttering detonation.

The blond newcomer slumped sidewise, his smoking gun falling from his fingers, a widening spot of crimson suddenly dyeing his shirt, his wide eyes fixed in sardonic self-mockery on the gun in O'Donnell's right hand.

"Corcoran!" he muttered. "I thought I had you fooled--you--"

Self-mocking laughter bubbled to his lips, cynical to the last; he was laughing as he died.

The man whose real name was Corcoran rose and looked down at his victim unemotionally. There was a hole in the side of his shirt, and a seared spot on the skin of his ribs burned like fire. Even with his aim spoiled by ripping lead, Glanton's bullet had passed close.

Reloading the empty chamber of his Colt, Corcoran started toward the horse the dead man had ridden up to the spring. He had taken but one step when a sound brought him around, the heavy Colt jumping back into his hand.

He scowled at the man who stood before him: a tall man, trimly built, and clad in frontier elegance.

"Don't shoot," this man said imperturbably. "I'm John Middleton, sheriff of Whapeton Gulch."

The warning attitude of the other did not relax.

"This was a private matter," he said.

"I guessed as much. Anyway, it's none of my business. I saw two men at the spring as I rode over a rise in the trail some distance back. I was only expecting one. I can't afford to take any chance. I left my horse a short distance back and came on afoot. I was watching from the bushes and saw the whole thing. He reached for his gun first, but you already had your hand almost on your gun. Your shot was first by a flicker. He fooled me. His move came as an absolute surprise to me."

"He thought it would to me," said Corcoran. "Billy Glanton always wanted the drop on his man. He always tried to get some advantage before he pulled his gun.

"He knew me as soon as he saw me; knew that I knew him. But he thought he was making me think that he didn't know me. I made him think that. He could take chances because he knew I wouldn't shoot him down without warnin'--which is just what he figured on doin' to me. Finally he thought he had me off my guard, and went for his gun. I was foolin' him all along."

Middleton looked at Corcoran with much interest. He was familiar with the two opposite breeds of gunmen. One kind was like Glanton; utterly cynical, courageous enough when courage was necessary, but always preferring to gain an advantage by treachery whenever possible. Corcoran typified the opposite breed; men too direct by nature, or too proud of their skill to resort to trickery when it was possible to meet their enemies in the open and rely on sheer speed and nerve and accuracy. But that Corcoran was a strategist was proved by his tricking Glanton into drawing.

Middleton looked down at Glanton; in death the yellow curls and boyish features gave the youthful gunman an appearance of innocence. But Middleton knew that that mask had covered the heart of a merciless grey wolf.

"A bad man!" he muttered, staring at the rows of niches on the ivory stock of Glanton's Colt.

"Plenty bad," agreed Corcoran. "My folks and his had a feud between 'em down in Texas. He came back from Kansas and killed an uncle of mine--shot him down in cold blood. I was in California when it happened. Got a letter a year after the feud was over. I was headin' for Kansas, where I figured he'd gone back to, when I met a man who told me he was in this part of the country, and was ridin' towards Whapeton. I cut his trail and camped here last night waitin' for him.

"It'd been years since we'd seen each other, but he knew me--didn't know I knew he knew me, though. That gave me the edge. You're the man he was goin' to meet here?"

"Yes. I need a gunfighting deputy bad. I'd heard of him. Sent him word."

Middleton's gaze wandered over Corcoran's hard frame, lingering on the guns at his hips.

"You pack two irons," remarked the sheriff. "I know what you can do with your right. But what about the left? I've seen plenty of men who wore two guns, but those who could use both I can count on my fingers."

"Well?"

15

"Well," smiled the sheriff, "I thought maybe you'd like to show what you can do with your left."

"Why do you think it makes any difference to me whether you believe I can handle both guns or not?" retorted Corcoran without heat.

Middleton seemed to like the reply.

"A tinhorn would be anxious to make me believe he could. You don't have to prove anything to me. I've seen enough to show me that you're the man I need. Corcoran, I came out here to hire Glanton as my deputy. I'll make the same proposition to you. What you were down in Texas, or out in California, makes no difference to me. I know your breed, and I know that you'll shoot square with a man who trusts you, regardless of what you may have been in other parts, or will be again, somewhere else.

"I'm up against a situation in Whapeton that I can't cope with alone, or with the forces I have.

"For a year the town and the camps up and down the gulch have been terrorized by a gang of outlaws who call themselves the Vultures.

"That describes them perfectly. No man's life or property is safe. Forty or fifty men have been murdered, hundreds robbed. It's next to impossible for a man to pack out any dust, or for a big shipment of gold to get through on the stage. So many men have been shot trying to protect shipments that the stage company has trouble hiring guards any more.

"Nobody knows who are the leaders of the gang. There are a number of ruffians who are suspected of being members of the Vultures, but we have no proof that would stand up, even in a miners' court. Nobody dares give evidence against any of them. When a man recognizes the men who rob him he doesn't dare reveal his knowledge. I can't get anyone to identify a criminal, though I know that robbers and murderers are walking the streets, and rubbing elbows with me along the bars. It's maddening! And yet I can't blame the poor devils. Any man who dared testify against one of them would be murdered.

"People blame me some, but I can't give adequate protection to the camp with the resources allowed me. You know how a gold camp is; everybody so greedy-blind they don't want to do anything but grab for the yellow dust. My deputies are brave men, but they can't be everywhere, and they're not gunfighters. If I arrest a man there are a dozen to stand up in a miners' court and swear enough lies to acquit him. Only last night they murdered one of my deputies, Jim Grimes, in cold blood.

"I sent for Billy Glanton when I heard he was in this country, because I need a man of more than usual skill. I need a man who can handle a gun like a streak of forked lightning, and knows all the tricks of trapping and killing a man. I'm tired of arresting criminals to be turned loose! Wild Bill Hickok has the right idea--kill the badmen and save the jails for the petty offenders!"

The Texan scowled slightly at the mention of Hickok, who was not loved by the riders who came up the cattle trails, but he nodded agreement with the sentiment expressed. The fact that he, himself, would fall into Hickok's category of those to be exterminated did not prejudice his viewpoint.

"You're a better man than Glanton," said Middleton abruptly. "The proof is that Glanton lies there dead, and here you stand very much alive. I'll offer you the same terms I meant to offer him."

He named a monthly salary considerably larger than that drawn by the average Eastern city marshal. Gold was the most plentiful commodity in Whapeton.

"And a monthly bonus," added Middleton. "When I hire talent I expect to pay for it; so do the merchants and miners who look to me for protection."

Corcoran meditated a moment.

"No use in me goin' on to Kansas now," he said finally. "None of my folks in Texas are havin' any feud that I know of. I'd like to see this Whapeton. I'll take you up."

"Good!" Middleton extended his hand and as Corcoran took it he noticed that it was much browner than the left. No glove had covered that hand for many years.

"Let's get it started right away! But first we'll have to dispose of Glanton's body."

"I'll take along his gun and horse and send 'em to Texas to his folks," said Corcoran.

"But the body?"

"Hell, the buzzards'll 'tend to it."

"No, no!" protested Middleton. "Let's cover it with bushes and rocks, at least."

Corcoran shrugged his shoulders. It was not vindictiveness which prompted his seeming callousness. His hatred of the blond youth did not extend to the lifeless body of the man. It was simply that he saw no use in going to what seemed to him an unnecessary task. He had hated Glanton with the merciless hate of his race, which is more enduring and more relentless than the hate of an Indian or a Spaniard. But toward the body that was no longer animated by the personality he had hated, he was simply indifferent. He expected some day to leave his own corpse stretched on the ground, and the thought of buzzards tearing at his dead flesh moved him no more than the sight of his dead enemy. His creed was pagan and nakedly elemental.

A man's body, once life had left it, was no more than any other carcass, moldering back into the soil which once produced it.

But he helped Middleton drag the body into an opening among the bushes, and build a rude cairn above it. And he waited patiently while Middleton carved the dead youth's name on a rude cross fashioned from broken branches, and thrust upright among the stones.

Then they rode for Whapeton, Corcoran leading the riderless roan; over the horn of the empty saddle hung the belt supporting the dead man's gun, the ivory stock of which bore eleven notches, each of which represented a man's life.

CHAPTER 2 GOLDEN MADNESS

The mining town of Whapeton sprawled in a wide gulch that wandered between sheer rock walls and steep hillsides. Cabins, saloons and dance-halls backed against the cliffs on the south side of the gulch. The houses facing them were almost on the bank of Whapeton Creek, which wandered down the gulch, keeping mostly to the center. On both sides of the creek cabins and tents straggled for a mile and a half each way from the main body of the town. Men were washing gold dust out of the creek, and out of its smaller tributaries which meandered into the canyon along tortuous ravines. Some of these ravines opened into the gulch between the houses built against the wall, and the cabins and tents which straggled up them gave the impression that the town had overflowed the main gulch and spilled into its tributaries.

Buildings were of logs, or of bare planks laboriously freighted over the mountains. Squalor and draggled or gaudy elegance rubbed elbows. An intense virility surged through the scene. What other qualities it might have lacked, it overflowed with a superabundance of vitality. Color, action, movement--growth and power! The atmosphere was alive with these elements, stinging and tingling. Here there were no delicate shadings or subtle contrasts. Life painted here in broad, raw colors, in bold, vivid strokes. Men who came here left behind them the delicate nuances, the cultured tranquilities of life. An empire was being built on muscle and guts and audacity, and men dreamed gigantically and wrought terrifically. No dream was too mad, no enterprise too tremendous to be accomplished.

Passions ran raw and turbulent. Boot heels stamped on bare plank floors, in the eddying dust of the street. Voices boomed, tempers exploded in sudden outbursts of primitive violence. Shrill voices of painted harpies mingled with the clank of gold on gambling tables, gusty mirth and vociferous altercation along the bars where raw liquor hissed in a steady stream down hairy, dust-caked throats. It was one of a thousand similar panoramas of the day, when a giant empire was bellowing in lusty infancy.

But a sinister undercurrent was apparent. Corcoran, riding by the sheriff, was aware of this, his senses and intuitions whetted to razor keenness by the life he led. The instincts of a gunfighter were developed to an abnormal alertness, else he had never lived out his first year of gunmanship. But it took no abnormally developed instinct to tell Corcoran that hidden currents ran here, darkly and strongly.

As they threaded their way among trains of pack-mules, rumbling wagons and swarms of men on foot which thronged the straggling street, Corcoran was aware of many eyes following them. Talk ceased suddenly among gesticulating groups as they recognized the sheriff, then the eyes swung to Corcoran, searching and appraising. He did not seem to be aware of their scrutiny.

Middleton murmured: "They know I'm bringing back a gunfighting deputy. Some of those fellows are Vultures, though I can't prove it. Look out for yourself."

Corcoran considered this advice too unnecessary to merit a reply. They were riding past the King of Diamonds gambling hall at the moment, and a group of men clustered in the doorway turned to stare at them. One lifted a hand in greeting to the sheriff.

"Ace Brent, the biggest gambler in the gulch," murmured Middleton as he returned the salute. Corcoran got a glimpse of a slim figure in elegant broadcloth, a keen, inscrutable countenance, and a pair of piercing black eyes.

Middleton did not enlarge upon his description of the man, but rode on in silence.

They traversed the body of the town--the clusters of stores and saloons--and passed on, halting at a cabin apart from the rest. Between it and the town the creek swung out in a wide loop that carried it some distance from the south wall of the gulch, and the cabins and tents straggled after the creek. That left this particular cabin isolated, for it was built with its back wall squarely against the sheer cliff. There was a corral on one side, a clump of trees on the other. Beyond the trees a narrow ravine opened into the gulch, dry and unoccupied.

"This is my cabin," said Middleton. "That cabin back there"--he pointed to one which they had passed, a few hundred yards back up the road--"I use for a sheriff's office. I need only one room. You can bunk in the back room. You can keep your horse in my corral, if you want to. I always keep several there for my deputies. It pays to have a fresh supply of horseflesh always on hand."

As Corcoran dismounted he glanced back at the cabin he was to occupy. It stood close to a clump of trees, perhaps a hundred yards from the steep wall of the gulch.

There were four men at the sheriff's cabin, one of which Middleton introduced to Corcoran as Colonel Hopkins, formerly of Tennessee. He was a tall, portly man with an iron grey mustache and goatee, as well dressed as Middleton himself.

"Colonel Hopkins owns the rich Elinor A. claim, in partnership with Dick Bisley," said Middleton; "in addition to being one of the most prominent merchants in the Gulch."

"A great deal of good either occupation does me, when I can't get my money out of town," retorted the colonel. "Three times my partner and I have lost big shipments of gold on the stage. Once we sent out a load concealed in wagons loaded with supplies supposed to be intended for the miners at Teton Gulch. Once clear of Whapeton the drivers were to swing back east through the mountains. But somehow the Vultures learned of our plan; they caught the wagons fifteen miles south of Whapeton, looted them and murdered the guards and drivers."

"The town's honeycombed with their spies," muttered Middleton.

"Of course. One doesn't know who to trust. It was being whispered in the streets that my men had been killed and robbed, before their bodies had been found. We know that the Vultures knew all about our plan, that they rode straight out from Whapeton, committed that crime and rode straight back with the gold dust. But we could do nothing. We can't prove anything, or convict anybody."

Middleton introduced Corcoran to the three deputies, Bill McNab, Richardson, and Stark. McNab was as tall as Corcoran and more heavily built, hairy and muscular, with restless eyes that reflected a violent temper. Richardson was more slender, with cold, unblinking eyes, and Corcoran instantly classified him as the most dangerous of the three. Stark was a burly, bearded fellow, not differing in type from hundreds of miners. Corcoran found the appearances of these men incongruous with their protestations of helplessness in the face of the odds against them. They looked like hard men, well able to take care of themselves in any situation.

Middleton, as if sensing his thoughts, said: "These men are not afraid of the devil, and they can throw a gun as quick as the average man, or quicker. But it's hard for a stranger to appreciate just what we're up against here in Whapeton. If it was a matter of an open fight, it would be different. I wouldn't need any more help. But it's blind going, working in the dark, not knowing who to trust. I don't dare to deputize a man unless I'm sure of his honesty. And who can be sure of who? We know the town is full of spies. We don't know who they are; we don't know who the leader of the Vultures is."

Hopkins' bearded chin jutted stubbornly as he said: "I still believe that gambler, Ace Brent, is mixed up with the gang. Gamblers have been murdered and robbed, but Brent's never been molested. What becomes of all the dust he wins? Many of the miners, despairing of ever getting out of the gulch with their gold, blow it all in the saloons and gambling halls. Brent's won thousands of dollars in dust and nuggets. So have several others. What becomes of it? It doesn't all go back into circulation. I believe they get it out, over the mountains. And if they do, when no one else can, that proves to my mind that they're members of the Vultures."

"Maybe they cache it, like you and the other merchants are doing," suggested Middleton. "I don't know. Brent's intelligent enough to be the chief of the Vultures. But I've never been able to get anything on him."

"You've never been able to get anything definite on anybody, except petty offenders," said Colonel Hopkins bluntly, as he took up his hat. "No offense intended, John.

We know what you're up against, and we can't blame you. But it looks like, for the good of the camp, we're going to have to take direct action."

Middleton stared after the broadcloth-clad back as it receded from the cabin.

"'We,'" he murmured. "That means the vigilantes--or rather the men who have been agitating a vigilante movement. I can understand their feelings, but I consider it an unwise move. In the first place, such an organization is itself outside the law, and would be playing into the hands of the lawless element. Then, what's to prevent outlaws from joining the vigilantes, and diverting it to suit their own ends?"

"Not a damned thing!" broke in McNab heatedly. "Colonel Hopkins and his friends are hot-headed. They expect too much from us. Hell, we're just ordinary workin' men. We do the best we can, but we ain't gunslingers like this man Corcoran here."

Corcoran found himself mentally questioning the whole truth of this statement; Richardson had all the earmarks of a gunman, if he had ever seen one, and the Texan's experience in such matters ranged from the Pacific to the Gulf.

Middleton picked up his hat. "You boys scatter out through the camp. I'm going to take Corcoran around, when I've sworn him in and given him his badge, and introduce him to the leading men of the camp.

"I don't want any mistake, or any chance of mistake, about his standing. I've put you in a tight spot, Corcoran, I'll admit--boasting about the gunfighting deputy I was going to get. But I'm confident that you can take care of yourself."

The eyes that had followed their ride down the street focused on the sheriff and his companion as they made their way on foot along the straggling street with its teeming saloons and gambling halls. Gamblers and bartenders were swamped with business, and merchants were getting rich with all commodities selling at unheard-of prices. Wages for day-labor matched prices for groceries, for few men could be found to toil for a prosaic, set salary when their eyes were dazzled by visions of creeks fat with yellow dust and gorges crammed with nuggets. Some of those dreams were not disappointed; millions of dollars in virgin gold was being taken out of the claims up and down the gulch. But the finders frequently found it a golden weight hung to their necks to drag them down to a bloody death. Unseen, unknown, on furtive feet the human wolves stole among them, unerringly marking their prey and striking in the dark.

From saloon to saloon, dance hall to dance hall, where weary girls in tawdry finery allowed themselves to be tussled and hauled about by bear-like males who emptied sacks of gold dust down the low necks of their dresses, Middleton piloted Corcoran, talking rapidly and incessantly. He pointed out men in the crowd and gave their names and status in the community, and introduced the Texan to the more important citizens of the camp.

All eyes followed Corcoran curiously. The day was still in the future when the northern ranges would be flooded by Texas cattle, driven by wiry Texas riders; but Texans were not unknown, even then, in the mining camps of the Northwest. In the first days of the gold rushes they had drifted in from the camps of California, to which, at a still earlier date, the Southwest had sent some of her staunchest and some of her most turbulent sons. And of late others had drifted in from the Kansas cattle towns along whose streets the lean riders were swaggering and fighting out feuds brought up from the far south country. Many in Whapeton were familiar with the characteristics of the Texas breed, and all had heard tales of the fighting men bred among the live oaks and mesquites of that hot, turbulent country where racial traits met and clashed, and the traditions of the Old South mingled with those of the untamed West.

Here, then, was a lean grey wolf from that southern pack; some of the men looked their scowling animosity; but most merely looked, in the role of spectators, eager to witness the drama all felt imminent.

"You're, primarily, to fight the Vultures, of course," Middleton told Corcoran as they walked together down the street. "But that doesn't mean you're to overlook petty offenders. A lot of small-time crooks and bullies are so emboldened by the success of the big robbers that they think they can get away with things, too. If you see a man shooting up a saloon, take his gun away and throw him into jail to sober up. That's the jail, up yonder at the other end of town. Don't let men fight on the street or in saloons. Innocent bystanders get hurt."

"All right." Corcoran saw no harm in shooting up saloons or fighting in public places. In Texas few innocent bystanders were ever hurt, for there men sent their bullets straight to the mark intended. But he was ready to follow instructions.

"So much for the smaller fry. You know what to do with the really bad men. We're not bringing any more murderers into court to be acquitted through their friends' lies!"

CHAPTER 3 GUNMAN'S TRAP

Night had fallen over the roaring madness that was Whapeton Gulch. Light streamed from the open doors of saloons and honky-tonks, and the gusts of noise that rushed out into the street smote the passers-by like the impact of a physical blow.

Corcoran traversed the street with the smooth, easy stride of perfectly poised muscles. He seemed to be looking straight ahead, but his eyes missed nothing on either side of him. As he passed each building in turn he analyzed the sounds that issued from the open door, and knew just how much was rough merriment and horseplay, recognized the elements of anger and menace when they edged some of the voices, and accurately appraised the extent and intensity of those emotions. A real gunfighter was not merely a man whose eye was truer, whose muscles were quicker than other men; he was a practical psychologist, a student of human nature, whose life depended on the correctness of his conclusions.

It was the Golden Garter dance hall that gave him his first job as a defender of law and order.

As he passed a startling clamor burst forth inside-- strident feminine shrieks piercing a din of coarse masculine hilarity. Instantly he was through the door and elbowing a way through the crowd which was clustered about the center of the room. Men cursed and turned belligerently as they felt his elbows in their ribs, twisted their heads to threaten him, and then gave back as they recognized the new deputy.

Corcoran broke through into the open space the crowd ringed, and saw two women fighting like furies. One, a tall, fine blond girl, had bent a shrieking, biting, clawing Mexican girl back over a billiard table, and the crowd was yelling joyful encouragement to one or the other: "Give it to her, Glory!" "Slug her, gal!" "Hell, Conchita, bite her!"

The brown girl heeded this last bit of advice and followed it so energetically that Glory cried out sharply and jerked away her wrist, which dripped blood. In the grip of the hysterical frenzy which seizes women in such moments, she caught up a billiard ball and lifted it to crash it down on the head of her screaming captive.

Corcoran caught that uplifted wrist, and deftly flicked the ivory sphere from her fingers. Instantly she whirled on him like a tigress, her yellow hair falling in disorder over her shoulders, bared by the violence of the struggle, her eyes blazing. She lifted her hands toward his face, her fingers working spasmodically, at which some drunk bawled, with a shout of laughter: "Scratch his eyes out, Glory!"

Corcoran made no move to defend his features; he did not seem to see the white fingers twitching so near his face. He was staring into her furious face, and the candid admiration of his gaze seemed to confuse her, even in her

32

anger. She dropped her hands but fell back on woman's traditional weapon--her tongue.

"You're Middleton's new deputy! I might have expected you to butt in! Where are McNab and the rest? Drunk in some gutter? Is this the way you catch murderers? You lawmen are all alike--better at bullying girls than at catching outlaws!"

Corcoran stepped past her and picked up the hysterical Mexican girl. Conchita seeing that she was more frightened than hurt, scurried toward the back rooms, sobbing in rage and humiliation, and clutching about her the shreds of garments her enemy's tigerish attack had left her.

Corcoran looked again at Glory, who stood clenching and unclenching her white fists. She was still fermenting with anger, and furious at his intervention. No one in the crowd about them spoke; no one laughed, but all seemed to hold their breaths as she launched into another tirade. They knew Corcoran was a dangerous man, but they did not know the code by which he had been reared; did not know that Glory, or any other woman, was safe from violence at his hands, whatever her offense.

"Why don't you call McNab?" she sneered. "Judging from the way Middleton's deputies have been working, it will probably take three or four of you to drag one helpless girl to jail!"

"Who said anything about takin' you to jail?" Corcoran's gaze dwelt in fascination on her ruddy cheeks, the crimson of her full lips in startling contrast against the whiteness of her teeth. She shook her yellow hair back impatiently, as a spirited young animal might shake back its flowing mane.

"You're not arresting me?" She seemed startled, thrown into confusion by this unexpected statement.

"No. I just kept you from killin' that girl. If you'd brained her with that billiard ball I'd have had to arrest you."

"She lied about me!" Her wide eyes flashed, and her breast heaved again.

"That wasn't no excuse for makin' a public show of yourself," he answered without heat. "If ladies have got to fight, they ought to do it in private."

And so saying he turned away. A gusty exhalation of breath seemed to escape the crowd, and the tension vanished, as they turned to the bar. The incident was forgotten, merely a trifling episode in an existence crowded with violent incidents. Jovial masculine voices mingled with the shriller laughter of women, as glasses began to clink along the bar.

Glory hesitated, drawing her torn dress together over her bosom, then darted after Corcoran, who was moving toward the door. When she touched his arm he whipped about as quick as a cat, a hand flashing to a gun. She glimpsed a momentary gleam in his eyes as menacing and predatory as the threat that leaps in a panther's eyes. Then it was gone as he saw whose hand had touched him.

"She lied about me," Glory said, as if defending herself from a charge of misconduct. "She's a dirty little cat."

Corcoran looked her over from head to foot, as if he had not heard her; his blue eyes burned her like a physical fire.

She stammered in confusion. Direct and unveiled admiration was commonplace, but there was an elemental candor about the Texan such as she had never before encountered.

He broke in on her stammerings in a way that showed he had paid no attention to what she was saying.

"Let me buy you a drink. There's a table over there where we can sit down."

"No. I must go and put on another dress. I just wanted to say that I'm glad you kept me from killing Conchita. She's a slut, but I don't want her blood on my hands."

"All right."

She found it hard to make conversation with him, and could not have said why she wished to make conversation.

"McNab arrested me once," she said, irrelevantly, her eyes dilating as if at the memory of an injustice. "I slapped him for something he said. He was going to put me in jail for resisting an officer of the law! Middleton made him turn me loose."

"McNab must be a fool," said Corcoran slowly.

"He's mean; he's got a nasty temper, and he--what's that?"

Down the street sounded a fusillade of shots, a blurry voice yelling gleefully.

"Some fool shooting up a saloon," she murmured, and darted a strange glance at her companion, as if a drunk shooting into the air was an unusual occurrence in that wild mining camp.

"Middleton said that's against the law," he grunted, turning away.

"Wait!" she cried sharply, catching at him. But he was already moving through the door, and Glory stopped short as a hand fell lightly on her shoulder from behind. Turning her head she paled to see the keenly-chiseled face of Ace Brent. His hand lay gently on her shoulder, but there was a command and a blood-chilling threat in its touch. She shivered and stood still as a statue, as Corcoran, unaware of the drama being played behind him, disappeared into the street.

The racket was coming from the Blackfoot Chief Saloon, a few doors down, and on the same side of the street as the Golden Garter. With a few long strides Corcoran reached the door. But he did not rush in. He halted and swept his cool gaze deliberately over the interior. In the center of the saloon a roughly dressed man was reeling about, whooping and discharging a pistol into the ceiling, perilously close to the big oil lamp which hung there. The bar was lined with men, all bearded and uncouthly garbed, so it was impossible to tell which were ruffians and which were honest miners. All the men in the room were at the bar, with the exception of the drunken man.

Corcoran paid little heed to him as he came through the door, though he moved straight toward him, and to the tense watchers it seemed the Texan was looking at no one else. In reality, from the corner of his eye he was watching the men at the bar; and as he moved deliberately from the door, across the room, he distinguished the pose of honest curiosity from the tension of intended murder. He saw the three hands that gripped gun butts.

And as he, apparently ignorant of what was going on at the bar, stepped toward the man reeling in the center of the room, a gun jumped from its scabbard and pointed toward the lamp. And even as it moved, Corcoran moved quicker. His turn was a blur of motion too quick for the eye to follow and even as he turned his gun was burning red.

The man who had drawn died on his feet with his gun still pointed toward the ceiling, unfired. Another stood gaping, stunned, a pistol dangling in his fingers, for that fleeting tick of time; then as he woke and whipped the gun up, hot lead ripped through his brain. A third gun spoke once as the owner fired wildly, and then he went to his knees under the blast of ripping lead, slumped over on the floor and lay twitching.

It was over in a flash, action so blurred with speed that not one of the watchers could ever tell just exactly what had happened. One instant Corcoran had been moving toward the man in the center of the room, the next both guns were blazing and three men were falling from the bar, crashing dead on the floor.

For an instant the scene held, Corcoran half-crouching, guns held at his hips, facing the men who stood stunned along the bar. Wisps of blue smoke drifted from the muzzles of his guns, forming a misty veil through which his grim face looked, implacable and passionless as that of an image carved from granite. But his eyes blazed.

Shakily, moving like puppets on a string, the men at the bar lifted their hands clear of their waistline. Death hung on the crook of a finger for a shuddering tick of time. Then with a choking gasp the man who had played drunk made a stumbling rush toward the door. With a catlike wheel and stroke Corcoran crashed a gun barrel over his head and stretched him stunned and bleeding on the floor.

The Texan was facing the men at the bar again before any of them could have moved. He had not looked at the men on the floor since they had fallen.

"Well, *amigos*!" His voice was soft, but it was thick with killer's lust. "Why don't you-all keep the *baile* goin'? Ain't these *hombres* got no friends?"

Apparently they had not. No one made a move.

Realizing that the crisis had passed, that there was no more killing to be done just then, Corcoran straightened, shoving his guns back in his scabbards.

"Purty crude," he criticized. "I don't see how anybody could fall for a trick that stale. Man plays drunk and starts shootin' at the roof. Officer comes in to arrest him. When the officer's back's turned, somebody shoots out the light, and the drunk falls on the floor to get out of the line of fire. Three or four men planted along the bar start blazin' away in the dark at the place where they know the law's standin', and out of eighteen or twenty-four shots, some's bound to connect."

With a harsh laugh he stooped, grabbed the "drunk" by the collar and hauled him upright. The man staggered and stared wildly about him, blood dripping from the gash in his scalp.

"You got to come along to jail," said Corcoran unemotionally. "Sheriff says it's against the law to shoot up saloons. I ought to shoot you, but I ain't in the habit of pluggin' men with empty guns. Reckon you'll be more value to the sheriff alive than dead, anyway."

And propelling his dizzy charge, he strode out into the street. A crowd had gathered about the door, and they gave back suddenly. He saw a supple, feminine figure dart into the circle of light, which illumined the white face and golden hair of the girl Glory.

"Oh!" she exclaimed sharply. "Oh!" Her exclamation was almost drowned in a sudden clamor of voices as the men in the street realized what had happened in the Blackfoot Chief.

Corcoran felt her pluck at his sleeve as he passed her, heard her tense whisper.

"I was afraid--I tried to warn you--I'm glad they didn't--"

A shadow of a smile touched his hard lips as he glanced down at her. Then he was gone, striding down the street toward the jail, half-pushing, half-dragging his bewildered prisoner.

CHAPTER 4 THE MADNESS THAT BLINDS MEN

Corcoran locked the door on the man who seemed utterly unable to realize just what had happened, and turned away, heading for the sheriff's office at the other end of town. He kicked on the door of the jailer's shack, a few yards from the jail, and roused that individual out of a slumber he believed was alcoholic, and informed him he had a prisoner in his care. The jailer seemed as surprised as the victim was.

No one had followed Corcoran to the jail, and the street was almost deserted, as the people jammed morbidly into the Blackfoot Chief to stare at the bodies and listen to conflicting stories as to just what had happened.

Colonel Hopkins came running up, breathlessly, to grab Corcoran's hand and pump it vigorously.

"By gad, sir, you have the real spirit! Guts! Speed! They tell me the loafers at the bar didn't even have time to dive for cover before it was over! I'll admit I'd ceased to expect much of John's deputies, but you've shown your metal! These fellows were undoubtedly Vultures. That Tom Deal, you've got in jail, I've suspected him for some time. We'll question him--make him tell us who the rest are, and who their leader is. Come in and have a drink, sir!"

"Thanks, but not just now. I'm goin' to find Middleton and report this business. His office ought to be closer to the jail. I don't think much of his jailer. When I get through reportin' I'm goin' back and guard that fellow myself."

Hopkins emitted more laudations, and then clapped the Texan on the back and darted away to take part in whatever informal inquest was being made, and Corcoran strode on through the emptying street. The fact that so much uproar was being made over the killing of three would-be murderers showed him how rare was a successful resistance to the Vultures. He shrugged his shoulders as he remembered feuds and range wars in his native Southwest: men falling like flies under the unerring drive of bullets on the open range and in the streets of Texas towns. But there all men were frontiersmen, sons and grandsons of frontiersmen; here, in the mining camps, the frontier element was only one of several elements, many drawn from sections where men had forgotten how to defend themselves through generations of law and order.

He saw a light spring up in the sheriff's cabin just before he reached it, and, with his mind on possible gunmen lurking in ambush--for they must have known he would go directly to the cabin from the jail--he swung about and approached the building by a route that would not take him across the bar of light pouring from the window. So it was that the man who came running noisily down the road passed him

42

without seeing the Texan as he kept in the shadows of the cliff. The man was McNab; Corcoran knew him by his powerful build, his slouching carriage. And as he burst through the door, his face was illuminated and Corcoran was amazed to see it contorted in a grimace of passion.

Voices rose inside the cabin, McNab's bull-like roar, thick with fury, and the calmer tones of Middleton. Corcoran hurried forward, and as he approached he heard McNab roar: "Damn you, Middleton, you've got a lot of explainin' to do! Why didn't you warn the boys he was a killer?"

At that moment Corcoran stepped into the cabin and demanded: "What's the trouble, McNab?"

The big deputy whirled with a feline snarl of rage, his eyes glaring with murderous madness as they recognized Corcoran.

"You damned--" A string of filthy expletives gushed from his thick lips as he ripped out his gun. Its muzzle had scarcely cleared leather when a Colt banged in Corcoran's right hand. McNab's gun clattered to the floor and he staggered back, grasping his right arm with his left hand, and cursing like a madman.

"What's the matter with you, you fool?" demanded Corcoran harshly. "Shut up! I did you a favor by not killin' you. If you wasn't a deputy I'd have drilled you through the head. But I will anyway, if you don't shut your dirty trap."

"You killed Breckman, Red Bill and Curly!" raved McNab; he looked like a wounded grizzly as he swayed there, blood trickling down his wrist and dripping off his fingers.

"Was that their names? Well, what about it?"

"Bill's drunk, Corcoran," interposed Middleton. "He goes crazy when he's full of liquor."

McNab's roar of fury shook the cabin. His eyes turned red and he swayed on his feet as if about to plunge at Middleton's throat.

"Drunk?" he bellowed. "You lie, Middleton! Damn you, what's your game? You sent your own men to death! Without warnin'!"

"His own men?" Corcoran's eyes were suddenly glittering slits. He stepped back and made a half-turn so that he was facing both men; his hands became claws hovering over his gun-butts.

"Yes, his men!" snarled McNab. "You fool, *he's* the chief of the Vultures!"

An electric silence gripped the cabin. Middleton stood rigid, his empty hands hanging limp, knowing that his life hung on a thread no more substantial than a filament of morning dew. If he moved, if, when he spoke, his tone jarred on Corcoran's suspicious ears, guns would be roaring before a man could snap his fingers.

"Is that so?" Corcoran shot at him.

"Yes," Middleton said calmly, with no inflection in his voice that could be taken as a threat. "I'm chief of the Vultures."

Corcoran glared at him puzzled. "What's your game?" he demanded, his tone thick with the deadly instinct of his breed.

"That's what I want to know!" bawled McNab. "We killed Grimes for you, because he was catchin' on to things. And we set the same trap for this devil. He knew! He must have known! You warned him--told him all about it!"

"He told me nothin'," grated Corcoran. "He didn't have to. Nobody but a fool would have been caught in a trap like that. Middleton, before I blow you to Hell, I want to know one thing: what good was it goin' to do you to bring me into Whapeton, and have me killed the first night I was here?"

"I didn't bring you here for that," answered Middleton.

"Then what'd you bring him here for?" yelled McNab. "You told us--"

"I told you I was bringing a new deputy here, that was a gunslinging fool," broke in Middleton. "That was the truth. That should have been warning enough."

"But we thought that was just talk, to fool the people," protested McNab bewilderedly. He sensed that he was beginning to be wound in a web he could not break.

"Did I tell you it was just talk?"

"No, but we thought--"

"I gave you no reason to think anything. The night when Grimes was killed I told everyone in the Golden Eagle that I was bringing in a Texas gunfighter as my deputy. I spoke the truth."

"But you wanted him killed, and--"

"I didn't. I didn't say a word about having him killed."

"But--"

"Did I?" Middleton pursued relentlessly. "Did I give you a definite order to kill Corcoran, to molest him in any way?"

Corcoran's eyes were molten steel, burning into McNab's soul. The befuddled giant scowled and floundered, vaguely realizing that he was being put in the wrong, but not understanding how, or why.

"No, you didn't tell us to kill him in so many words; but you didn't tell us to let him alone."

"Do I have to tell you to let people alone to keep you from killing them? There are about three thousand people in this camp I've never given any definite orders about. Are you going out and kill them, and say you thought I meant you to do it, because I didn't tell you not to?"

"Well, I--" McNab began apologetically, then burst out in righteous though bewildered wrath: "Damn it, it was the understandin' that we'd get rid of deputies like that, who wasn't on the inside. We thought you were bringin' in an honest deputy to fool the folks, just like you hired Jim Grimes to fool 'em. We thought you was just makin' a talk to the fools in the Golden Eagle. We thought you'd want him out of the way as quick as possible--"

"You drew your own conclusions and acted without my orders," snapped Middleton. "That's all that it amounts to. Naturally Corcoran defended himself. If I'd had any idea that you fools would try to murder him, I'd have passed the word to let him alone. I thought you understood my motives. I brought Corcoran in here to fool the people; yes. But he's not a man like Jim Grimes. Corcoran is with us. He'll clean out the thieves that are working outside our gang, and we'll accomplish two things with one stroke: get rid of competition and make the miners think we're on the level."

McNab stood glaring at Middleton; three times he opened his mouth, and each time he shut it without speaking. He knew that an injustice had been done him; that a responsibility that was not rightfully his had been dumped on his brawny shoulders. But the subtle play of Middleton's wits was beyond him; he did not know how to defend himself or make a countercharge.

"All right," he snarled. "We'll forget it. But the boys ain't goin' to forget how Corcoran shot down their pards. I'll talk to 'em, though. Tom Deal's got to be out of that jail before daylight. Hopkins is aimin' to question him about the gang. I'll stage a fake jailbreak for him. But first I've got to get this arm dressed." And he slouched out of the cabin and away through the darkness, a baffled giant, burning with murderous rage, but too tangled in a net of subtlety to know where or how or who to smite.

Back in the cabin Middleton faced Corcoran who still stood with his thumbs hooked in his belt, his fingers near his gun butts. A whimsical smile played on Middleton's thin lips, and Corcoran smiled back; but it was the mirthless grin of a crouching panther.

"You can't tangle me up with words like you did that big ox," Corcoran said. "You let me walk into that trap. You knew your men were ribbin' it up. You let 'em go ahead, when a word from you would have stopped it. You knew they'd think you wanted me killed, like Grimes, if you didn't say nothin'. You let 'em think that, but you played safe by not givin' any definite orders, so if anything went wrong, you could step out from under and shift the blame onto McNab."

Middleton smiled appreciatively, and nodded coolly.

"That's right. All of it. You're no fool, Corcoran."

Corcoran ripped out an oath, and this glimpse of the passionate nature that lurked under his inscrutable exterior was like a momentary glimpse of an enraged cougar, eyes blazing, spitting and snarling.

"Why?" he exclaimed. "Why did you plot all this for me? If you had a grudge against Glanton, I can understand why you'd rib up a trap for him, though you wouldn't have had no more luck with him than you have with me. But you ain't got no feud against me. I never saw you before this mornin'!"

"I have no feud with you; I had none with Glanton. But if Fate hadn't thrown you into my path, it would have been Glanton who would have been ambushed in the Blackfoot Chief. Don't you see, Corcoran? It was a test. I had to be sure you were the man I wanted."

Corcoran scowled, puzzled himself now.

"What do you mean?"

"Sit down!" Middleton himself sat down on a nearby chair, unbuckled his gun-belt and threw it, with the heavy, holstered gun, onto a table, out of easy reach. Corcoran seated himself, but his vigilance did not relax, and his gaze rested on Middleton's left arm pit, where a second gun might be hidden.

"In the first place," said Middleton, his voice flowing tranquilly, but pitched too low to be heard outside the cabin, "I'm chief of the Vultures, as that fool said. I organized them, even before I was made sheriff. Killing a robber and murderer, who was working outside my gang, made the people of Whapeton think I'd make a good sheriff. When they gave me the office, I saw what an advantage it would be to me and my gang.

"Our organization is airtight. There are about fifty men in the gang. They are scattered throughout these mountains. Some pose as miners; some are gamblers--Ace Brent, for instance. He's my right-hand man. Some work in saloons, some clerk in stores. One of the regular drivers of the stage-line company is a Vulture, and so is a clerk of the company, and one of the men who works in the company's stables, tending the horses.

"With spies scattered all over the camp, I know who's trying to take out gold, and when. It's a cinch. We can't lose."

"I don't see how the camp stands for it," grunted Corcoran.

"Men are too crazy after gold to think about anything else. As long as a man isn't molested himself, he doesn't care much what happens to his neighbors. We are organized; they are not. We know who to trust; they don't. It can't last forever. Sooner or later the more intelligent citizens will organize themselves into a vigilante committee and sweep the gulch clean. But when that happens, I intend to be far away--with one man I can trust."

Corcoran nodded, comprehension beginning to gleam in his eyes.

"Already some men are talking vigilante. Colonel Hopkins, for instance. I encourage him as subtly as I can."

"Why, in the name of Satan?"

"To avert suspicion; and for another reason. The vigilantes will serve my purpose at the end."

"And your purpose is to skip out and leave the gang holdin' the sack!"

"Exactly! Look here!"

Taking the candle from the table, he led the way through a back room, where heavy shutters covered the one window. Shutting the door, he turned to the back wall and drew aside some skins which were hung over it. Setting the candle on a roughly hewed table, he fumbled at the logs, and a section swung outward, revealing a heavy plank door set in the solid rock against which the back wall of the cabin was built. It was braced with iron and showed a ponderous lock. Middleton produced a key, and turned it in the lock, and pushed the door inward. He lifted the candle and revealed a small cave, lined and heaped with canvas and buckskin sacks. One of these sacks had burst open, and a golden stream caught the glints of the candle.

"Gold! Sacks and sacks of it!"

Corcoran caught his breath, and his eyes glittered like a wolf's in the candlelight. No man could visualize the contents of those bags unmoved. And the gold-madness had long ago entered Corcoran's veins, more powerfully than he had dreamed, even though he had followed the lure to California and back over the mountains again. The sight of that glittering heap, of those bulging sacks, sent his pulses pounding in his temples, and his hand unconsciously locked on the butt of a gun.

"There must be a million there!"

"Enough to require a good-sized mule-train to pack it out," answered Middleton. "You see why I have to have a man to help me the night I pull out. And I need a man like you. You're an outdoor man, hardened by wilderness travel. You're a frontiersman, a *vaquero*, a trail-driver. These men I lead are mostly rats that grew up in border towns-- gamblers, thieves, barroom gladiators, saloon-bred gunmen; a few miners gone wrong. You can stand things that would kill any of them.

"The flight we'll have to make will be hard traveling. We'll have to leave the beaten trails and strike out through the mountains. They'll be sure to follow us, and we'll probably have to fight them off. Then there are Indians--Blackfeet and Crows; we may run into a war party of them. I knew I had to have a fighting man of the keenest type; not only a fighting man, but a man bred on the frontier. That's why I sent for Glanton. But you're a better man than he was."

Corcoran frowned his suspicion.

"Why didn't you tell me all this at first?"

"Because I wanted to try you out. I wanted to be sure you were the right man. I had to be sure. If you were stupid enough, and slow enough to be caught in such a trap as

McNab and the rest would set for you, you weren't the man I wanted."

"You're takin' a lot for granted," snapped Corcoran. "How do you know I'll fall in with you and help you loot the camp and then double-cross your gang? What's to prevent me from blowin' your head off for the trick you played on me? Or spillin' the beans to Hopkins, or to McNab?"

"Half a million in gold!" answered Middleton. "If you do any of those things, you'll miss your chance to share that cache with me."

He shut the door, locked it, pushed the other door to and hung the skins over it. Taking the candle he led the way back into the outer room.

He seated himself at the table and poured whisky from a jug into two glasses.

"Well, what about it?"

Corcoran did not at once reply. His brain was still filled with blinding golden visions. His countenance darkened, became sinister as he meditated, staring into his whisky glass.

The men of the West lived by their own code. The line between the outlaw and the honest cattleman or *vaquero* was sometimes a hair line, too vague to always be traced with accuracy. Men's personal codes were frequently inconsistent, but rigid as iron. Corcoran would not have stolen one cow, or three cows from a squatter, but he had swept across the border to loot Mexican *rancherios* of hundreds of head. He would not hold up a man and take his money, nor would he murder a man in cold blood; but he felt no compunctions about killing a thief and taking the money the thief had stolen. The gold in that cache was bloodstained, the fruit of crimes to which he would have scorned to stoop. But his code of honesty did not prevent him from looting it from the thieves who had looted it in turn from honest men.

"What's my part in the game?" Corcoran asked abruptly.

Middleton grinned zestfully.

"Good! I thought you'd see it my way. No man could look at that gold and refuse a share of it! They trust me more than they do any other member of the gang. That's why I keep it here. They know--or think they know--that I couldn't slip out with it. But that's where we'll fool them.

"Your job will be just what I told McNab: you'll uphold law and order. I'll tell the boys not to pull any more holdups inside the town itself, and that'll give you a reputation. People will think you've got the gang too scared to work in close. You'll enforce laws like those against shooting up saloons, fighting on the street, and the like. And you'll catch the thieves that are still working alone. When you kill one we'll make it appear that he was a Vulture. You've put yourself solid with the people tonight, by killing those fools in the Blackfoot Chief. We'll keep up the deception.

"I don't trust Ace Brent. I believe he's secretly trying to usurp my place as chief of the gang. He's too damned smart. But I don't want you to kill him. He has too many friends in the gang. Even if they didn't suspect I put you up to it, even if it looked like a private quarrel, they'd want your scalp. I'll frame him--get somebody outside the gang to kill him, when the time comes.

"When we get ready to skip, I'll set the vigilantes and the Vultures to battling each other--how, I don't know, but I'll find a way--and we'll sneak while they're at it. Then for California--South America and the sharing of the gold!"

"The sharin' of the gold!" echoed Corcoran, his eyes lit with grim laughter.

Their hard hands met across the rough table, and the same enigmatic smile played on the lips of both men.

CHAPTER 5 THE WHEEL BEGINS TO TURN

Corcoran stalked through the milling crowd that swarmed in the street, and headed toward the Golden Garter Dance Hall and Saloon. A man lurching through the door with the wide swing of hilarious intoxication stumbled into him and clutched at him to keep from falling to the floor.

Corcoran righted him, smiling faintly into the bearded, rubicund countenance that peered into his.

"Steve Corcoran, by thunder!" whooped the inebriated one gleefully. "Besh damn' deputy in the Territory! 'S' a honor to get picked up by Steve Corcoran! Come in and have a drink."

"You've had too many now," returned Corcoran.

"Right!" agreed the other. "I'm goin' home now, 'f I can get there. Lasht time I was a little full, I didn't make it, by a quarter of a mile! I went to sleep in a ditch across from your shack. I'd 'a' come in and slept on the floor, only I was 'fraid you'd shoot me for one of them derned Vultures!"

Men about them laughed. The intoxicated man was Joe Willoughby, a prominent merchant in Whapeton, and extremely popular for his free-hearted and open-handed ways.

"Just knock on the door next time and tell me who it is," grinned Corcoran. "You're welcome to a blanket in the

56

sheriff's office, or a bunk in my room, any time you need it."

"Soul of gener--generoshity!" proclaimed Willoughby boisterously. "Goin' home now before the licker gets down in my legs. S'long, old pard!"

He weaved away down the street, amidst the jovial joshings of the miners, to which he retorted with bibulous good nature.

Corcoran turned again into the dance hall and brushed against another man, at whom he glanced sharply, noting the set jaw, the haggard countenance and the bloodshot eyes. This man, a young miner well known to Corcoran, pushed his way through the crowd and hurried up the street with the manner of a man who goes with a definite purpose. Corcoran hesitated, as though to follow him, then decided against it and entered the dance hall. Half the reason for a gunfighter's continued existence lay in his ability to read and analyze the expressions men wore, to correctly interpret the jut of jaw, the glitter of eye. He knew this young miner was determined on some course of action that might result in violence. But the man was not a criminal, and Corcoran never interfered in private quarrels so long as they did not threaten the public safety.

A girl was singing, in a clear, melodious voice, to the accompaniment of a jangling, banging piano. As Corcoran seated himself at a table, with his back to the wall and a clear view of the whole hall before him, she concluded her number amid a boisterous clamor of applause. Her face lit as she saw him. Coming lightly across the hall, she sat down at his table. She rested her elbows on the table, cupped her chin in her hands, and fixed her wide clear gaze on his brown face.

"Shot any Vultures today, Steve?"

He made no answer as he lifted the glass of beer brought him by a waiter.

"They must be scared of you," she continued, and something of youthful hero-worship glowed in her eyes. "There hasn't been a murder or holdup in town for the past month, since you've been here. Of course you can't be everywhere. They still kill men and rob them in the camps up the ravines, but they keep out of town.

"And that time you took the stage through to Yankton! It wasn't your fault that they held it up and got the gold on the other side of Yankton. You weren't in it, then. I wish I'd been there and seen the fight, when you fought off the men who tried to hold you up, halfway between here and Yankton."

"There wasn't any fight to it," he said impatiently, restless under praise he knew he did not deserve.

"I know; they were afraid of you. You shot at them and they ran."

Very true; it had been Middleton's idea for Corcoran to take the stage through to the next town east, and beat off a fake attempt at holdup. Corcoran had never relished the memory; whatever his faults, he had the pride of his profession; a fake gunfight was as repugnant to him as a business hoax to an honest business man.

"Everybody knows that the stage company tried to hire you away from Middleton, as a regular shotgun-guard. But you told them that your business was to protect life and property here in Whapeton."

She meditated a moment and then laughed reminiscently.

"You know, when you pulled me off of Conchita that night, I thought you were just another blustering bully like McNab. I was beginning to believe that Middleton was taking pay from the Vultures, and that his deputies were crooked. I know things that some people don't." Her eyes became shadowed as if by an unpleasant memory in which, though her companion could not know it, was limned the handsome, sinister face of Ace Brent. "Or maybe people do. Maybe they guess things, but are afraid to say anything.

"But I was mistaken about you, and since you're square, then Middleton must be, too. I guess it was just too big a job for him and his other deputies. None of them could have wiped out that gang in the Blackfoot Chief that night like you did. It wasn't your fault that Tom Deal got away that night, before he could be questioned. If he hadn't though, maybe you could have made him tell who the other Vultures were."

"I met Jack McBride comin' out of here," said Corcoran abruptly. "He looked like he was about ready to start gunnin' for somebody. Did he drink much in here?"

"Not much. I know what's the matter with him. He's been gambling too much down at the King of Diamonds. Ace Brent has been winning his money for a week. McBride's nearly broke, and I believe he thinks Brent is crooked. He came in here, drank some whisky, and let fall a remark about having a showdown with Brent."

Corcoran rose abruptly. "Reckon I better drift down towards the King of Diamonds. Somethin' may bust loose there. McBride's quick with a gun, and high tempered. Brent's deadly. Their private business is none of my affair. But if they want to fight it out, they'll have to get out where innocent people won't get hit by stray slugs."

Glory Bland watched him as his tall, erect figure swung out of the door, and there was a glow in her eyes that had never been awakened there by any other man.

Corcoran had almost reached the King of Diamonds gambling hall, when the ordinary noises of the street were split by the crash of a heavy gun. Simultaneously men came headlong out of the doors, shouting, shoving, plunging in their haste.

"McBride's killed!" bawled a hairy miner.

"No, it's Brent!" yelped another. The crowd surged and milled, craning their necks to see through the windows, yet crowding back from the door in fear of stray bullets. As Corcoran made for the door he heard a man bawl in answer to an eager question: "McBride accused Brent of usin' marked cards, and offered to prove it to the crowd. Brent said he'd kill him and pulled his gun to do it. But it snapped. I heard the hammer click. Then McBride drilled him before he could try again."

Men gave way as Corcoran pushed through the crowd. Somebody yelped: "Look out, Steve! McBride's on the warpath!"

Corcoran stepped into the gambling hall, which was deserted except for the gambler who lay dead on the floor, with a bullet-hole over his heart, and the killer who half-crouched with his back to the bar, and a smoking gun lifted in his hand.

McBride's lips were twisted hard in a snarl, and he looked like a wolf at bay.

"Get back, Corcoran," he warned. "I ain't got nothin' against you, but I ain't goin' to be murdered like a sheep."

"Who said anything about murderin' you?" demanded Corcoran impatiently.

"Oh, I know you wouldn't. But Brent's got friends. They'll never let me get away with killin' him. I believe he was a Vulture. I believe the Vultures will be after me for this. But if they get me, they've got to get me fightin'."

"Nobody's goin' to hurt you," said Corcoran tranquilly. "You better give me your gun and come along. I'll have to arrest you, but it won't amount to nothin', and you ought to know it. As soon as a miners' court can be got together, you'll be tried and acquitted. It was a plain case of self-defense. I reckon no honest folks will do any grievin' for Ace Brent."

"But if I give up my gun and go to jail," objected McBride, wavering, "I'm afraid the toughs will take me out and lynch me."

"I'm givin' you my word you won't be harmed while you're under arrest," answered Corcoran.

"That's enough for me," said McBride promptly, extending his pistol.

Corcoran took it and thrust it into his waistband. "It's damned foolishness, takin' an honest man's gun," he grunted. "But accordin' to Middleton that's the law. Give me your word that you won't skip, till you've been properly acquitted, and I won't lock you up."

"I'd rather go to jail," said McBride. "I wouldn't skip. But I'll be safer in jail, with you guardin' me, than I would be walkin' around loose for some of Brent's friends to shoot me in the back. After I've been cleared by due process of law, they won't dare to lynch me, and I ain't afraid of 'em when it comes to gunfightin', in the open."

"All right." Corcoran stooped and picked up the dead gambler's gun, and thrust it into his belt. The crowd surging about the door gave way as he led his prisoner out.

"There the skunk is!" bawled a rough voice. "He murdered Ace Brent!"

McBride turned pale with anger and glared into the crowd, but Corcoran urged him along, and the miner grinned as other voices rose: "A damned good thing, too!" "Brent was crooked!" "He was a Vulture!" bawled somebody, and for a space a tense silence held. That charge was too sinister to bring openly against even a dead man. Frightened by his own indiscretion the man who had shouted slunk away, hoping none had identified his voice.

"I've been gamblin' too much," growled McBride, as he strode along beside Corcoran. "Afraid to try to take my gold out, though, and didn't know what else to do with it. Brent won thousands of dollars worth of dust from me; poker, mostly.

"This mornin' I was talkin' to Middleton, and he showed a card he said a gambler dropped in his cabin last night. He showed me it was marked, in a way I'd never have suspected. I recognized it as one of the same brand Brent always uses, though Middleton wouldn't tell me who the gambler was. But later I learned that Brent slept off a drunk in Middleton's cabin. Damned poor business for a gambler to get drunk.

"I went to the King of Diamonds awhile ago, and started playin' poker with Brent and a couple of miners. As soon as he raked in the first pot, I called him--flashed the card I got from Middleton and started to show the boys where it was marked. Then Brent pulled his gun; it snapped, and I killed him before he could cock it again. He knew I had the goods on him. He didn't even give me time to tell where I'd gotten the card."

Corcoran made no reply. He locked McBride in the jail, called the jailer from his nearby shack and told him to furnish the prisoner with food, liquor and anything else he needed, and then hurried to his own cabin. Sitting on his bunk in the room behind the sheriff's office, he ejected the cartridge on which Brent's pistol had snapped. The cap was dented, but had not detonated the powder. Looking closely he saw faint abrasions on both the bullet and brass case. They were such as might have been made by the jaws of iron pinchers and a vise.

Securing a wire-cutter with pincher jaws, he began to work at the bullet. It slipped out with unusual ease, and the contents of the case spilled into his hand. He did not need to use a match to prove that it was not powder. He knew what the stuff was at first glance--iron filings, to give the proper weight to the cartridge from which the powder had been removed.

At that moment he heard someone enter the outer room, and recognized the firm, easy tread of Sheriff Middleton. Corcoran went into the office and Middleton turned, hung his white hat on a nail.

"McNab tells me McBride killed Ace Brent!"

"You ought to know!" Corcoran grinned. He tossed the bullet and empty case on the table, dumped the tiny pile of iron dust beside them.

"Brent spent the night with you. You got him drunk, and stole one of his cards to show to McBride. You knew how his cards were marked. You took a cartridge out of Brent's gun and put that one in place. One would be enough. You knew there'd be gunplay between him and McBride, when you showed McBride that marked card, and you wanted to be sure it was Brent who stopped lead."

"That's right," agreed Middleton. "I haven't seen you since early yesterday morning. I was going to tell you about the frame I'd ribbed, as soon as I saw you. I didn't know McBride would go after Brent as quickly as he did.

"Brent got too ambitious. He acted as if he were suspicious of us both, lately. Maybe, though, it was just jealousy as far as you were concerned. He liked Glory Bland, and she could never see him. It gouged him to see her falling for you.

"And he wanted my place as leader of the Vultures. If there was one man in the gang that could have kept us from skipping with the loot, it was Ace Brent.

"But I think I've worked it neatly. No one can accuse me of having him murdered, because McBride isn't in the gang. I have no control over him. But Brent's friends will want revenge."

"A miners' court will acquit McBride on the first ballot."

"That's true. Maybe we'd better let him get shot, trying to escape!"

"We will like hell!" rapped Corcoran. "I swore he wouldn't be harmed while he was under arrest. His part of the deal was on the level. He didn't know Brent had a blank in his gun, any more than Brent did. If Brent's friends want his scalp, let 'em go after McBride, like white men ought to, when he's in a position to defend himself."

"But after he's acquitted," argued Middleton, "they won't dare gang up on him in the street, and he'll be too sharp to give them a chance at him in the hills."

"What the hell do I care?" snarled Corcoran. "What difference does it make to me whether Brent's friends get even or not? Far as I'm concerned, he got what was comin' to him. If they ain't got the guts to give McBride an even break, I sure ain't goin' to fix it so they can murder him without riskin' their own hides. If I catch 'em sneakin' around the jail for a shot at him, I'll fill 'em full of hot lead.

"If I'd thought the miners would be crazy enough to do anything to him for killin' Brent, I'd never arrested him. They won't. They'll acquit him. Until they do, I'm responsible for him, and I've give my word. And anybody that tries to lynch him while he's in my charge better be damned sure they're quicker with a gun than I am."

"There's nobody of that nature in Whapeton," admitted Middleton with a wry smile. "All right, if you feel your personal honor is involved. But I'll have to find a way to placate Brent's friends, or they'll be accusing me of being indifferent about what happened to him."

CHAPTER 6 VULTURES' COURT

Next morning Corcoran was awakened by a wild shouting in the street. He had slept in the jail that night, not trusting Brent's friends, but there had been no attempt at violence. He jerked on his boots, and went out into the street, followed by McBride, to learn what the shouting was about.

Men milled about in the street, even at that early hour--for the sun was not yet up--surging about a man in the garb of a miner. This man was astride a horse whose coat was dark with sweat; the man was wild eyed, bareheaded, and he held his hat in his hands, holding it down for the shouting, cursing throng to see.

"Look at 'em!" he yelled. "Nuggets as big as hen eggs! I took 'em out in an hour, with a pick, diggin' in the wet sand by the creek! And there's plenty more! It's the richest strike these hills ever seen!"

"Where?" roared a hundred voices.

"Well, I got my claim staked out, all I need," said the man, "so I don't mind tellin' you. It ain't twenty miles from here, in a little canyon everybody's overlooked and passed over--Jackrabbit Gorge! The creek's buttered with dust, and the banks are crammed with pockets of nuggets!"

An exuberant whoop greeted this information, and the crowd broke up suddenly as men raced for their shacks.

"New strike," sighed McBride enviously. "The whole town will be surgin' down Jackrabbit Gorge. Wish I could go."

"Gimme your word you'll come back and stand trial, and you can go," promptly offered Corcoran. McBride stubbornly shook his head.

"No, not till I've been cleared legally. Anyway, only a handful of men will get anything. The rest will be pullin' back into their claims in Whapeton Gulch tomorrow. Hell, I've been in plenty of them rushes. Only a few ever get anything."

Colonel Hopkins and his partner Dick Bisley hurried past. Hopkins shouted: "We'll have to postpone your trial until this rush is over, Jack! We were going to hold it today, but in an hour there won't be enough men in Whapeton to impanel a jury! Sorry you can't make the rush. If we can, Dick and I will stake out a claim for you!"

"Thanks, Colonel!"

"No thanks! The camp owes you something for ridding it of that scoundrel Brent. Corcoran, we'll do the same for you, if you like."

"No, thanks," drawled Corcoran. "Minin's too hard work. I've got a gold mine right here in Whapeton that don't take so much labor!"

The men burst into laughter at this conceit, and Bisley shouted back as they hurried on: "That's right! Your salary looks like an assay from the Comstock lode! But you earn it, all right!"

Joe Willoughby came rolling by, leading a seedy-looking burro on which illy-hung pick and shovel banged against skillet and kettle. Willoughby grasped a jug in one hand, and that he had already been sampling it was proved by his wide-legged gait.

"H'ray for the new diggin's!" he whooped, brandishing the jug at Corcoran and McBride. "Git along, jackass! I'll be scoopin' out nuggets bigger'n this jug before night--if the licker don't git in my legs before I git there!"

"And if it does, he'll fall into a ravine and wake up in the mornin' with a fifty pound nugget in each hand," said McBride. "He's the luckiest son of a gun in the camp; and the best natured."

"I'm goin' and get some ham-and-eggs," said Corcoran. "You want to come and eat with me, or let Pete Daley fix your breakfast here?"

"I'll eat in the jail," decided McBride. "I want to stay in jail till I'm acquitted. Then nobody can accuse me of tryin' to beat the law in any way."

"All right." With a shout to the jailer, Corcoran swung across the road and headed for the camp's most pretentious restaurant, whose proprietor was growing rich, in spite of the terrific prices he had to pay for vegetables and food of all kinds--prices he passed on to his customers.

While Corcoran was eating, Middleton entered hurriedly, and bending over him, with a hand on his shoulder, spoke softly in his ear.

"I've just got wind that that old miner, Joe Brockman, is trying to sneak his gold out on a pack mule, under the pretense of making this rush. I don't know whether it's so or not, but some of the boys up in the hills think it is, and are planning to waylay him and kill him. If he intends getting away, he'll leave the trail to Jackrabbit Gorge a few miles out of town, and swing back toward Yankton, taking the trail over Grizzly Ridge--you know where the thickets are so close. The boys will be laying for him either on the ridge or just beyond.

"He hasn't enough dust to make it worth our while to take it. If they hold him up they'll have to kill him, and we want as few murders as possible. Vigilante sentiment is growing, in spite of the people's trust in you and me. Get on your horse and ride to Grizzly Ridge and see that the old man gets away safe. Tell the boys Middleton said to lay off. If they won't listen--but they will. They wouldn't buck you, even without my word to back you. I'll follow the old man, and try to catch up with him before he leaves the Jackrabbit Gorge road.

"I've sent McNab up to watch the jail, just as a formality. I know McBride won't try to escape, but we mustn't be accused of carelessness."

"Let McNab be mighty careful with his shootin' irons," warned Corcoran. "No 'shot while attemptin' to escape', Middleton. I don't trust McNab. If he lays a hand on McBride, I'll kill him as sure as I'm sittin' here."

"Don't worry. McNab hated Brent. Better get going. Take the short cut through the hills to Grizzly Ridge."

"Sure." Corcoran rose and hurried out in the street which was all but deserted. Far down toward the other end of the gulch rose the dust of the rearguard of the army which was surging toward the new strike. Whapeton looked almost like a deserted town in the early morning light, foreshadowing its ultimate destiny.

Corcoran went to the corral beside the sheriff's cabin and saddled a fast horse, glancing cryptically at the powerful pack mules whose numbers were steadily increasing. He smiled grimly as he remembered Middleton telling Colonel Hopkins that pack mules were a good investment. As he led his horse out of the corral his gaze fell on a man sprawling under the trees across the road, lazily whittling. Day and night, in one way or another, the gang kept an eye on the cabin which hid the cache of their gold. Corcoran doubted if they actually suspected Middleton's intentions. But they wanted to be sure that no stranger did any snooping about.

Corcoran rode into a ravine that straggled away from the gulch, and a few minutes later he followed a narrow path to its rim, and headed through the mountains toward the spot, miles away, where a trail crossed Grizzly Ridge, a long, steep backbone, thickly timbered.

He had not left the ravine far behind him when a quick rattle of hoofs brought him around, in time to see a horse slide recklessly down a low bluff amid a shower of shale. He swore at the sight of its rider.

"Glory! What the hell?"

"Steve!" She reined up breathlessly beside him. "Go back! It's a trick! I heard Buck Gorman talking to Conchita; he's sweet on her. He's a friend of Brent's--a Vulture! She twists all his secrets out of him. Her room is next to mine, she thought I was out. I overheard them talking. Gorman said a trick had been played on you to get you out of town. He didn't say how. Said you'd go to Grizzly Ridge on a wild-goose chase. While you're gone they're going to assemble a 'miners' court,' out of the riff-raff left in town. They're going to appoint a 'judge' and 'jury,' take McBride out of jail, try him for killing Ace Brent--and hang him!"

A lurid oath ripped through Steve Corcoran's lips, and for an instant the tiger flashed into view, eyes blazing, fangs bared. Then his dark face was an inscrutable mask again. He wrenched his horse around.

"Much obliged, Glory. I'll be dustin' back into town. You circle around and come in another way. I don't want folks to know you told me."

"Neither do I!" she shuddered. "I knew Ace Brent was a Vulture. He boasted of it to me, once when he was drunk. But I never dared tell anyone. He told me what he'd do to me if I did. I'm glad he's dead. I didn't know Gorman was a Vulture, but I might have guessed it. He was Brent's closest friend. If they ever find out I told you--"

"They won't," Corcoran assured her. It was natural for a girl to fear such black-hearted rogues as the Vultures, but the thought of them actually harming her never entered his mind. He came from a country where not even the worst of scoundrels would ever dream of hurting a woman.

He drove his horse at a reckless gallop back the way he had come, but not all the way. Before he reached the Gulch he swung wide of the ravine he had followed out, and plunged into another, that would bring him into the Gulch at the end of town where the jail stood. As he rode down it he heard a deep, awesome roar he recognized--the roar of the man-pack, hunting its own kind.

A band of men surged up the dusty street, roaring, cursing. One man waved a rope. Pale faces of bartenders, store clerks and dance hall girls peered timidly out of doorways as the unsavory mob roared past. Corcoran knew them, by sight or reputation: plug-uglies, barroom loafers, skulkers--

many were Vultures, as he knew; others were riff-raff, ready for any sort of deviltry that required neither courage nor intelligence--the scum that gathers in any mining camp.

Dismounting, Corcoran glided through the straggling trees that grew behind the jail, and heard McNab challenge the mob.

"What do you want?"

"We aim to try your prisoner!" shouted the leader. "We come in the due process of law. We've app'inted a jedge and paneled a jury, and we demands that you hand over the prisoner to be tried in miners' court, accordin' to legal precedent!"

"How do I know you're representative of the camp?" parried McNab.

"'Cause we're the only body of men in camp right now!" yelled someone, and this was greeted by a roar of laughter.

"We come empowered with the proper authority--" began the leader, and broke off suddenly: "Grab him, boys!"

There was the sound of a brief scuffle, McNab swore vigorously, and the leader's voice rose triumphantly: "Let go of him, boys, but don't give him his gun. McNab, you ought to know better'n to try to oppose legal procedure, and you a upholder of law and order!"

Again a roar of sardonic laughter, and McNab growled: "All right; go ahead with the trial. But you do it over my protests. I don't believe this is a representative assembly."

"Yes, it is," averred the leader, and then his voice thickened with blood-lust. "Now, Daley, gimme that key and bring out the prisoner."

The mob surged toward the door of the jail, and at that instant Corcoran stepped around the corner of the cabin and leaped up on the low porch it boasted. There was a hissing intake of breath. Men halted suddenly, digging their heels against the pressure behind them. The surging line wavered backward, leaving two figures isolated--McNab, scowling, disarmed, and a hairy giant whose huge belly was girt with a broad belt bristling with gun butts and knife hilts. He held a noose in one hand, and his bearded lips gaped as he glared at the unexpected apparition.

For a breathless instant Corcoran did not speak. He did not look at McBride's pallid countenance peering through the barred door behind him. He stood facing the mob, his head slightly bent, a somber, immobile figure, sinister with menace.

"Well," he said finally, softly, "what's holdin' up the *baile?*"

The leader blustered feebly.

"We come here to try a murderer!"

Corcoran lifted his head and the man involuntarily recoiled at the lethal glitter of his eyes.

"Who's your judge?" the Texan inquired softly.

"We appointed Jake Bissett, there," spoke up a man, pointing at the uncomfortable giant on the porch.

"So you're goin' to hold a miners' court," murmured Corcoran. "With a judge and jury picked out of the dives and honky-tonks--scum and dirt of the gutter!" And suddenly uncontrollable fury flamed in his eyes. Bissett, sensing his intention, bellowed in ox-like alarm and grabbed frantically at a gun. His fingers had scarcely touched the checkered butt when smoke and flame roared from Corcoran's right hip. Bissett pitched backward off the porch as if he had been struck by a hammer; the rope tangled about his limbs as he fell, and he lay in the dust that slowly turned crimson, his hairy fingers twitching spasmodically.

Corcoran faced the mob, livid under his sun-burnt bronze. His eyes were coals of blue hell's-fire. There was a gun in each hand, and from the right-hand muzzle a wisp of blue smoke drifted lazily upward.

"I declare this court adjourned!" he roared. "The judge is done impeached, and the jury's discharged! I'll give you thirty seconds to clear the courtroom!"

He was one man against nearly a hundred, but he was a grey wolf facing a pack of yapping jackals. Each man knew that if the mob surged on him, they would drag him down at last; but each man knew what an awful toll would first be paid, and each man feared that he himself would be one of those to pay that toll.

They hesitated, stumbled back--gave way suddenly and scattered in all directions. Some backed away, some shamelessly turned their backs and fled. With a snarl Corcoran thrust his guns back in their scabbards and turned toward the door where McBride stood, grasping the bars.

"I thought I was a goner that time, Corcoran," he gasped. The Texan pulled the door open, and pushed McBride's pistol into his hand.

"There's a horse tied behind the jail," said Corcoran. "Get on it and dust out of here. I'll take the full responsibility. If you stay here they'll burn down the jail, or shoot you through the window. You can make it out of town while they're scattered. I'll explain to Middleton and Hopkins. In a month or so, if you want to, come back and stand trial, as a matter of formality. Things will be cleaned up around here by then."

McBride needed no urging. The grisly fate he had just escaped had shaken his nerve. Shaking Corcoran's hand passionately, he ran stumblingly through the trees to the horse Corcoran had left there. A few moments later he was fogging it out of the Gulch.

McNab came up, scowling and grumbling.

"You had no authority to let him go. I tried to stop the mob--"

Corcoran wheeled and faced him, making no attempt to conceal his hatred.

"You did like hell! Don't pull that stuff with me, McNab. You was in on this, and so was Middleton. You put up a bluff of talk, so afterwards you could tell Colonel Hopkins and the others that you tried to stop the lynchin' and was overpowered. I saw the scrap you put up when they grabbed you! Hell! You're a rotten actor."

"You can't talk to me like that!" roared McNab.

The old tigerish light flickered in the blue eyes. Corcoran did not exactly move, yet he seemed to sink into a half-crouch, as a cougar does for the killing spring.

"If you don't like my style, McNab," he said softly, thickly, "you're more'n welcome to open the *baile* whenever you get ready!"

For an instant they faced each other, McNab black browed and scowling, Corcoran's thin lips almost smiling, but blue fire lighting his eyes. Then with a grunt McNab turned and slouched away, his shaggy head swaying from side to side like that of a surly bull.

CHAPTER 7 A VULTURE'S WINGS ARE CLIPPED

Middleton pulled up his horse suddenly as Corcoran reined out of the bushes. One glance showed the sheriff that Corcoran's mood was far from placid. They were amidst a grove of alders, perhaps a mile from the Gulch.

"Why, hello, Corcoran," began Middleton, concealing his surprise. "I caught up with Brockman. It was just a wild rumor. He didn't have any gold. That--"

"Drop it!" snapped Corcoran. "I know why you sent me off on that wild-goose chase--same reason you pulled out of town. To give Brent's friends a chance to get even with McBride. If I hadn't turned around and dusted back into Whapeton, McBride would be kickin' his life out at the end of a rope, right now."

"You came back--?"

"Yeah! And now Jake Bissett's in Hell instead of Jack McBride, and McBride's dusted out--on a horse I gave him. I told you I gave him my word he wouldn't be lynched."

"You killed Bissett?"

"Deader'n hell!"

"He was a Vulture," muttered Middleton, but he did not seem displeased. "Brent, Bissett--the more Vultures die, the easier it will be for us to get away when we go. That's one reason I had Brent killed. But you should have let them hang McBride. Of course I framed this affair; I had to do something to satisfy Brent's friends. Otherwise they might have gotten suspicious.

"If they suspicioned I had anything to do with having him killed, or thought I wasn't anxious to punish the man who killed him, they'd make trouble for me. I can't have a split in the gang now. And even I can't protect you from Brent's friends, after this."

"Have I ever asked you, or any man, for protection?" The quick jealous pride of the gunfighter vibrated in his voice.

"Breckman, Red Bill, Curly, and now Bissett. You've killed too many Vultures. I made them think the killing of the first three was a mistake, all around. Bissett wasn't very popular. But they won't forgive you for stopping them from hanging the man who killed Ace Brent. They won't attack you openly, of course. But you'll have to watch every step you make. They'll kill you if they can, and I won't be able to prevent them."

"If I'd tell 'em just how Ace Brent died, you'd be in the same boat," said Corcoran bitingly. "Of course, I won't. Our final getaway depends on you keepin' their confidence--as well as the confidence of the honest folks. This last killin' ought to put me, and therefore you, ace-high with Hopkins and his crowd."

"They're still talking vigilante. I encourage it. It's coming anyway. Murders in the outlying camps are driving men to a frenzy of fear and rage, even though such crimes have ceased in Whapeton. Better to fall in line with the inevitable and twist it to a man's own ends, than to try to oppose it. If you can keep Brent's friends from killing you for a few more weeks, we'll be ready to jump. Look out for Buck Gorman. He's the most dangerous man in the gang. He was Brent's friend, and he has his own friends--all dangerous men. Don't kill him unless you have to."

"I'll take care of myself," answered Corcoran somberly. "I looked for Gorman in the mob, but he wasn't there. Too smart. But he's the man behind the mob. Bissett was just a stupid ox; Gorman planned it--or rather, I reckon he helped you plan it."

"I'm wondering how you found out about it," said Middleton. "You wouldn't have come back unless somebody told you. Who was it?"

"None of your business," growled Corcoran. It did not occur to him that Glory Bland would be in any danger from Middleton, even if the sheriff knew about her part in the affair, but he did not relish being questioned, and did not feel obliged to answer anybody's queries.

"That new gold strike sure came in mighty handy for you and Gorman," he said. "Did you frame that, too?"

Middleton nodded.

"Of course. That was one of my men who poses as a miner. He had a hatful of nuggets from the cache. He served his purpose and joined the men who hide up there in the hills. The mob of miners will be back tomorrow, tired and mad and disgusted, and when they hear about what happened, they'll recognize the handiwork of the Vultures; at least some of them will. But they won't connect me with it in any way. Now we'll ride back to town. Things are breaking our way, in spite of your foolish interference with the mob. But let Gorman alone. You can't afford to make any more enemies in the gang."

Buck Gorman leaned on the bar in the Golden Eagle and expressed his opinion of Steve Corcoran in no uncertain terms. The crowd listened sympathetically, for, almost to a man, they were the ruffians and riff-raff of the camp.

"The dog pretends to be a deputy!" roared Gorman, whose bloodshot eyes and damp tangled hair attested to the amount of liquor he had drunk. "But he kills an appointed judge, breaks up a court and drives away the jury--yes, and releases the prisoner, a man charged with murder!"

It was the day after the fake gold strike, and the disillusioned miners were drowning their chagrin in the saloons. But few honest miners were in the Golden Eagle.

"Colonel Hopkins and other prominent citizens held an investigation," said someone. "They declared that evidence showed Corcoran to have been justified--denounced the court as a mob, acquitted Corcoran of killing Bissett, and then went ahead and acquitted McBride for killing Brent, even though he wasn't there."

Gorman snarled like a cat, and reached for his whisky glass. His hand did not twitch or quiver, his movements were more catlike than ever. The whisky had inflamed his mind, illumined his brain with a white-hot certainty that was akin to insanity, but it had not affected his nerves or any part of his muscular system. He was more deadly drunk than sober.

"I was Brent's best friend!" he roared. "I was Bissett's friend."

"They say Bissett was a Vulture," whispered a voice. Gorman lifted his tawny head and glared about the room as a lion might glare.

"Who says he was a Vulture? Why don't these slanderers accuse a living man? It's always a dead man they accuse! Well, what if he was? He was my friend! Maybe that makes *me* a Vulture!"

No one laughed or spoke as his flaming gaze swept the room, but each man, as those blazing eyes rested on him in turn, felt the chill breath of Death blowing upon him.

"Bissett a Vulture!" he said, wild enough with drink and fury to commit any folly, as well as any atrocity. He did not heed the eyes fixed on him, some in fear, a few in intense interest. "Who knows who the Vultures are? Who knows who, or what anybody really is? Who really knows anything about this man Corcoran, for instance? I could tell--"

A light step on the threshold brought him about as Corcoran loomed in the door. Gorman froze, snarling, lips writhed back, a tawny-maned incarnation of hate and menace.

"I heard you was makin' a talk about me down here, Gorman," said Corcoran. His face was bleak and emotionless as that of a stone image, but his eyes burned with murderous purpose.

Gorman snarled wordlessly.

"I looked for you in the mob," said Corcoran, tonelessly, his voice as soft and without emphasis as the even strokes of a feather. It seemed almost as if his voice were a thing apart from him; his lips murmuring while all the rest of his being was tense with concentration on the man before him.

"You wasn't there. You sent your coyotes, but you didn't have the guts to come yourself, and--"

The dart of Gorman's hand to his gun was like the blurring stroke of a snake's head, but no eye could follow Corcoran's hand. His gun smashed before anyone knew he had reached for it. Like an echo came the roar of Gorman's shot. But the bullet ploughed splinteringly into the floor, from a hand that was already death-stricken and falling. Gorman pitched over and lay still, the swinging lamp glinting on his upturned spurs and the blue steel of the smoking gun which lay by his hand.

CHAPTER 8 THE COMING OF THE VIGILANTES

Colonel Hopkins looked absently at the liquor in his glass, stirred restlessly, and said abruptly: "Middleton, I might as well come to the point. My friends and I have organized a vigilante committee, just as we should have done months ago. Now, wait a minute. Don't take this as a criticism of your methods. You've done wonders in the last month, ever since you brought Steve Corcoran in here. Not a holdup in the town, not a killing--that is, not a murder, and only a few shootings among the honest citizens.

"Added to that the ridding of the camp of such scoundrels as Jake Bissett and Buck Gorman. They were both undoubtedly members of the Vultures. I wish Corcoran hadn't killed Gorman just when he did, though. The man was drunk, and about to make some reckless disclosures about the gang. At least that's what a friend of mine thinks, who was in the Golden Eagle that night. But anyway it couldn't be helped.

"No, we're not criticizing you at all. But obviously you can't stop the murders and robberies that are going on up and down the Gulch, all the time. And you can't stop the outlaws from holding up the stage regularly.

"So that's where we come in. We have sifted the camp, carefully, over a period of months, until we have fifty men we can trust absolutely. It's taken a long time, because we've had to be sure of our men. We didn't want to take in a man who might be a spy for the Vultures. But at last we know where we stand. We're not sure just who *is* a Vulture, but we know who *isn't*, in as far as our organization is concerned.

"We can work together, John. We have no intention of interfering within your jurisdiction, or trying to take the law out of your hands. We demand a free hand outside the camp; inside the limits of Whapeton we are willing to act under your orders, or at least according to your advice. Of course we will work in absolute secrecy until we have proof enough to strike."

"You must remember, Colonel," reminded Middleton, "that all along I've admitted the impossibility of my breaking up the Vultures with the limited means at my disposal. I've never opposed a vigilante committee. All I've demanded was that when it was formed, it should be composed of honest men, and be free of any element which might seek to twist its purpose into the wrong channels."

"That's true. I didn't expect any opposition from you, and I can assure you that we'll always work hand-in-hand with you and your deputies." He hesitated, as if over something unpleasant, and then said: "John, are you sure of *all* your deputies?"

Middleton's head jerked up and he shot a startled glance at the Colonel, as if the latter had surprised him by putting into words a thought that had already occurred to him.

"Why do you ask?" he parried.

"Well," Hopkins was embarrassed, "I don't know--maybe I'm prejudiced--but--well, damn it, to put it bluntly, I've sometimes wondered about Bill McNab!"

Middleton filled the glasses again before he answered.

"Colonel, I never accuse a man without iron-clad evidence. I'm not always satisfied with McNab's actions, but it may merely be the man's nature. He's a surly brute. But he has his virtues. I'll tell you frankly, the reason I haven't discharged him is that I'm not sure of him. That probably sounds ambiguous."

"Not at all. I appreciate your position. You have as much as said you suspect him of double-dealing, and are keeping him on your force so you can watch him. Your wits are not dull, John. Frankly--and this will probably surprise you--until a month ago some of the men were beginning to whisper some queer things about you--queer suspicions, that is. But your bringing Corcoran in showed us that you were on the level. You'd have never brought him in if you'd been taking pay from the Vultures!"

Middleton halted with his glass at his lips.

"Great heavens!" he ejaculated. "Did they suspect me of *that*?"

"Just a fool idea some of the men had," Hopkins assured him. "Of course I never gave it a thought. The men who thought it are ashamed now. The killing of Bissett, of Gorman, of the men in the Blackfoot Chief, show that Corcoran's on the level. And of course, he's merely taking his orders from you. All those men were Vultures, of course. It's a pity Tom Deal got away before we could question him." He rose to go.

"McNab was guarding Deal," said Middleton, and his tone implied more than his words said.

Hopkins shot him a startled glance.

"By heaven, so he was! But he was really wounded--I saw the bullet hole in his arm, where Deal shot him in making his getaway."

"That's true." Middleton rose and reached for his hat. "I'll walk along with you. I want to find Corcoran and tell him what you've just told me."

"It's been a week since he killed Gorman," mused Hopkins. "I've been expecting Gorman's Vulture friends to try to get him, any time."

"So have I!" answered Middleton, with a grimness which his companion missed.

CHAPTER 9 THE VULTURES SWOOP

Down the gulch lights blazed; the windows of cabins were yellow squares in the night, and beyond them the velvet sky reflected the lurid heart of the camp. The intermittent breeze brought faint strains of music and the other noises of hilarity. But up the gulch, where a clump of trees straggled near an unlighted cabin, the darkness of the moonless night was a mask that the faint stars did not illuminate.

Figures moved in the deep shadows of the trees, voices whispered, their furtive tones mingling with the rustling of the wind through the leaves.

"We ain't close enough. We ought to lay alongside his cabin and blast him as he goes in."

A second voice joined the first, muttering like a bodyless voice in a conclave of ghosts.

"We've gone all over that. I tell you this is the best way. Get him off guard. You're sure Middleton was playin' cards at the King of Diamonds?"

Another voice answered: "He'll be there till daylight, likely."

"He'll be awful mad," whispered the first speaker.

"Let him. He can't afford to do anything about it. *Listen!* Somebody's comin' up the road!"

They crouched down in the bushes, merging with the blacker shadows. They were so far from the cabin, and it was so dark, that the approaching figure was only a dim blur in the gloom.

"It's him!" a voice hissed fiercely, as the blur merged with the bulkier shadow that was the cabin.

In the stillness a door rasped across a sill. A yellow light sprang up, streaming through the door, blocking out a small window high up in the wall. The man inside did not cross the lighted doorway, and the window was too high to see through into the cabin.

The light went out after a few minutes.

"Come on!" The three men rose and went stealthily toward the cabin. Their bare feet made no sound, for they had discarded their boots. Coats too had been discarded, any garment that might swing loosely and rustle, or catch on projections. Cocked guns were in their hands, they could have been no more wary had they been approaching the lair of a lion. And each man's heart pounded suffocatingly, for the prey they stalked was far more dangerous than any lion.

When one spoke it was so low that his companions hardly heard him with their ears a matter of inches from his bearded lips.

"We'll take our places like we planned, Joel. You'll go to the door and call him, like we told you. He knows Middleton trusts you. He don't know you'd be helpin' Gorman's friends.

He'll recognize your voice, and he won't suspect nothin'. When he comes to the door and opens it, step back into the shadows and fall flat. We'll do the rest from where we'll be layin'."

His voice shook slightly as he spoke, and the other man shuddered; his face was a pallid oval in the darkness.

"I'll do it, but I bet he kills some of us. I bet he kills me, anyway. I must have been crazy when I said I'd help you fellows."

"You can't back out now!" hissed the other. They stole forward, their guns advanced, their hearts in their mouths. Then the foremost man caught at the arms of his companions.

"Wait! Look there! He's left the door open!"

The open doorway was a blacker shadow in the shadow of the wall.

"He knows we're after him!" There was a catch of hysteria in the babbling whisper. "It's a trap!"

"Don't be a fool! How could he know? He's asleep. I hear him snorin'. We won't wake him. We'll step into the cabin and let him have it! We'll have enough light from the window to locate the bunk, and we'll rake it with lead before he can move. He'll wake up in Hell. Come on, and for God's sake, don't make no noise!"

The last advice was unnecessary. Each man, as he set his bare foot down, felt as if he were setting it into the lair of a diamond-backed rattler.

As they glided, one after another, across the threshold, they made less noise than the wind blowing through the black branches. They crouched by the door, straining their eyes across the room, whence came the rhythmic snoring. Enough light sifted through the small window to show them a vague outline that was a bunk, with a shapeless mass upon it.

A man caught his breath in a short, uncontrollable gasp. Then the cabin was shaken by a thunderous volley, three guns roaring together. Lead swept the bunk in a devastating storm, thudding into flesh and bone, smacking into wood. A wild cry broke in a gagging gasp. Limbs thrashed wildly and a heavy body tumbled to the floor. From the darkness on the floor beside the bunk welled up hideous sounds, choking gurgles and a convulsive flopping and thumping. The men crouching near the door poured lead blindly at the sounds. There was fear and panic in the haste and number of their shots. They did not cease jerking their triggers until their guns were empty, and the noises on the floor had ceased.

"Out of here, quick!" gasped one.

"No! Here's the table, and a candle on it. I felt it in the dark. I've got to *know* that he's dead before I leave this cabin. I've got to see him lyin' dead if I'm goin' to sleep easy. We've got plenty of time to get away. Folks down the gulch must have heard the shots, but it'll take time for them to get here. No danger. I'm goin' to light the candle--"

There was a rasping sound, and a yellow light sprang up, etching three staring, bearded faces. Wisps of blue smoke blurred the light as the candle wick ignited from the fumbling match, but the men saw a huddled shape crumpled near the bunk, from which streams of dark crimson radiated in every direction.

"Ahhh!"

They whirled at the sound of running footsteps.

"Oh, God!" shrieked one of the men, falling to his knees, his hands lifted to shut out a terrible sight. The other ruffians staggered with the shock of what they saw. They stood gaping, livid, helpless, empty guns sagging in their hands.

For in the doorway, glaring in dangerous amazement, with a gun in each hand, stood the man whose lifeless body they thought lay over there by the splintered bunk!

"Drop them guns!" Corcoran rasped. They clattered on the floor as the hands of their owner mechanically reached skyward. The man on the floor staggered up, his hands empty; he retched, shaken by the nausea of fear.

"Joel Miller!" said Corcoran evenly; his surprise was passed, as he realized what had happened. "Didn't know you run with Gorman's crowd. Reckon Middleton'll be some surprised, too."

"You're a devil!" gasped Miller. "You can't be killed! We killed you--heard you roll off your bunk and die on the floor, in the dark. We kept shooting after we knew you were dead. But you're alive!"

"You didn't shoot me," grunted Corcoran. "You shot a man you thought was me. I was comin' up the road when I heard the shots. You killed Joe Willoughby! He was drunk and I reckon he staggered in here and fell in my bunk, like he's done before."

The men went whiter yet under their bushy beards, with rage and chagrin and fear.

"Willoughby!" babbled Miller. "The camp will never stand for this! Let us go, Corcoran! Hopkins and his crowd will hang us! It'll mean the end of the Vultures! Your end, too, Corcoran! If they hang us, we'll talk first! They'll find out that you're one of us!"

"In that case," muttered Corcoran, his eyes narrowing, "I'd better kill the three of you. That's the sensible solution. You killed Willoughby, tryin' to get me; I kill you, in self-defense."

"Don't do it, Corcoran!" screamed Miller, frantic with terror.

"Shut up, you dog," growled one of the other men, glaring balefully at their captor. "Corcoran wouldn't shoot down unarmed men."

"No, I wouldn't," said Corcoran. "Not unless you made some kind of a break. I'm peculiar that way, which I see is a handicap in this country. But it's the way I was raised, and I can't get over it. No, I ain't goin' to beef you cold, though you've just tried to get me that way.

"But I'll be damned if I'm goin' to let you sneak off, to come back here and try it again the minute you get your nerve bucked up. I'd about as soon be hanged by the vigilantes as shot in the back by a passle of rats like you-all. Vultures, hell! You ain't even got the guts to be good buzzards.

"I'm goin' to take you down the gulch and throw you in jail. It'll be up to Middleton to decide what to do with you. He'll probably work out some scheme that'll swindle everybody except himself; but I warn you--one yap about the Vultures to anybody, and I'll forget my raisin' and send you to Hell with your belts empty and your boots on."

The noise in the King of Diamonds was hushed suddenly as a man rushed in and bawled: "The Vultures have murdered Joe Willoughby! Steve Corcoran caught three of 'em, and has just locked 'em up! This time we've got some live Vultures to work on!"

A roar answered him and the gambling hall emptied itself as men rushed yelling into the street. John Middleton laid down his hand of cards, donned his white hat with a hand that was steady as a rock, and strode after them.

Already a crowd was surging and roaring around the jail. The miners were lashed into a murderous frenzy and were restrained from shattering the door and dragging forth the cowering prisoners only by the presence of Corcoran, who faced them on the jail-porch. McNab, Richardson and Stark were there, also. McNab was pale under his whiskers, and Stark seemed nervous and ill at ease, but Richardson, as always, was cold as ice.

"Hang 'em!" roared the mob. "Let us have 'em, Steve! You've done your part! This camp's put up with enough! Let us have 'em!"

Middleton climbed up on the porch, and was greeted by loud cheers, but his efforts to quiet the throng proved futile. Somebody brandished a rope with a noose in it. Resentment, long smoldering, was bursting into flame, fanned by hysterical fear and hate. The mob had no wish to harm either Corcoran or Middleton--did not intend to harm them. But they were determined to drag out the prisoners and string them up.

Colonel Hopkins forced his way through the crowd, mounted the step, and waved his hands until he obtained a certain amount of silence.

"Listen, men!" he roared, "this is the beginning of a new era for Whapeton! This camp has been terrorized long enough. We're beginning a rule of law and order, right now! But don't spoil it at the very beginning! These men shall hang--I swear it! But let's do it legally, and with the sanction of law. Another thing: if you hang them out of hand, we'll never learn who their companions and leaders are.

"Tomorrow, I promise you, a court of inquiry will sit on their case. They'll be questioned and forced to reveal the men above and behind them. This camp is going to be cleaned up! Let's clean it up lawfully and in order!"

"Colonel's right!" bawled a bearded giant. "Ain't no use to hang the little rats till we find out who's the big 'uns!"

A roar of approbation rose as the temper of the mob changed. It began to break up, as the men scattered to hasten back to the bars and indulge in their passion to discuss the new development.

Hopkins shook Corcoran's hand heartily.

"Congratulations, sir! I've seen poor Joe's body. A terrible sight. The fiends fairly shot the poor fellow to ribbons. Middleton, I told you the vigilantes wouldn't usurp your authority in Whapeton. I keep my word. We'll leave these murderers in your jail, guarded by your deputies. Tomorrow the vigilante court will sit in session, and I hope we'll come to the bottom of this filthy mess."

And so saying he strode off, followed by a dozen or so steely-eyed men whom Middleton knew formed the nucleus of the Colonel's organization.

When they were out of hearing, Middleton stepped to the door and spoke quickly to the prisoners: "Keep your mouths shut. You fools have gotten us all in a jam, but I'll snake you out of it, somehow." To McNab he spoke: "Watch the jail. Don't let anybody come near it. Corcoran and I have got to talk this over." Lowering his voice so the prisoners could not hear, he added: "If anybody does come, that you can't order off, and these fools start shooting off their heads, close their mouths with lead."

Corcoran followed Middleton into the shadow of the gulch wall. Out of earshot of the nearest cabin, Middleton turned. "Just what happened?"

"Gorman's friends tried to get me. They killed Joe Willoughby by mistake. I hauled them in. That's all."

"That's not all," muttered Middleton. "There'll be hell to pay if they come to trial. Miller's yellow. He'll talk, sure. I've been afraid Gorman's friends would try to kill you-- wondering how it would work out. It's worked out just about the worst way it possibly could. You should either have killed them or let them go. Yet I appreciate your attitude. You have scruples against cold-blooded murder; and if you'd turned them loose, they'd have been back potting at you the next night."

"I couldn't have turned them loose if I'd wanted to. Men had heard the shots; they came runnin'; found me there holdin' a gun on those devils, and Joe Willoughby's body layin' on the floor, shot to pieces."

"I know. But we can't keep members of our own gang in jail, and we can't hand them over to the vigilantes. I've got to delay that trial, somehow. If I were ready, we'd jump tonight, and to hell with it. But I'm not ready. After all, perhaps it's as well this happened. It may give us our chance to skip. We're one jump ahead of the vigilantes and the gang, too. We know the vigilantes have formed and are ready to strike, and the rest of the gang don't. I've told no one but you what Hopkins told me early in the evening.

"Listen, Corcoran, we've got to move tomorrow night! I wanted to pull one last job, the biggest of all--the looting of Hopkins and Bisley's private cache. I believe I could have done it, in spite of all their guards and precautions. But we'll have to let that slide. I'll persuade Hopkins to put off the trial another day. I think I know how. Tomorrow night I'll have the vigilantes and the Vultures at each others' throats! We'll load the mules and pull out while they're fighting. Once let us get a good start, and they're welcome to chase us if they want to.

"I'm going to find Hopkins now. You get back to the jail. If McNab talks to Miller or the others, be sure you listen to what's said."

Middleton found Hopkins in the Golden Eagle Saloon.

"I've come to ask a favor of you, Colonel," he began directly. "I want you, if it's possible, to put off the investigating trial until day after tomorrow. I've been talking to Joel Miller. He's cracking. If I can get him away from Barlow and Letcher, and talk to him, I believe he'll tell me everything I want to know. It'll be better to get his confession, signed and sworn to, before we bring the matter into court. Before a judge, with all eyes on him, and his friends in the crowd, he might stiffen and refuse to incriminate anyone. I don't believe the others will talk. But talking to me, alone, I believe Miller will spill the whole works. But it's going to take time to wear him down. I believe that by tomorrow night I'll have a full confession from him."

"That would make our work a great deal easier," admitted Hopkins.

"And another thing: these men ought to be represented by proper counsel. You'll prosecute them, of course; and the only other lawyer within reach is Judge Bixby, at Yankton. We're doing this thing in as close accordance to regular legal procedure as possible. Therefore we can't refuse the prisoner the right to be defended by an attorney. I've sent a man after Bixby. It will be late tomorrow evening before he can get back with the Judge, even if he has no trouble in locating him.

"Considering all these things, I feel it would be better to postpone the trial until we can get Bixby here, and until I can get Miller's confession."

"What will the camp think?"

"Most of them are men of reason. The few hotheads who might want to take matters into their own hands can't do any harm."

"All right," agreed Hopkins. "After all, they're your prisoners, since your deputy captured them, and the attempted murder of an officer of the law is one of the charges for which they'll have to stand trial. We'll set the trial for day after tomorrow. Meanwhile, work on Joel Miller. If we have his signed confession, naming the leaders of the gang, it will expedite matters a great deal at the trial."

CHAPTER 10 THE BLOOD ON THE GOLD

Whapeton learned of the postponement of the trial and reacted in various ways. The air was surcharged with tension. Little work was done that day. Men gathering in heated, gesticulating groups, crowded in at the bars. Voices rose in hot altercation, fists pounded on the bars. Unfamiliar faces were observed, men who were seldom seen in the gulch- -miners from claims in distant canyons, or more sinister figures from the hills, whose business was less obvious.

Lines of cleavage were noticed. Here and there clumps of men gathered, keeping to themselves and talking in low tones. In certain dives the ruffian element of the camp gathered, and these saloons were shunned by honest men. But still the great mass of the people milled about, suspicious and uncertain. The status of too many men was still in doubt. Certain men were known to be above suspicion, certain others were known to be ruffians and criminals; but between these two extremes there were possibilities for all shades of distrust and suspicion.

So most men wandered aimlessly to and fro, with their weapons ready to their hands, glancing at their fellows out of the corners of their eyes.

To the surprise of all, Steve Corcoran was noticed at several bars, drinking heavily, though the liquor did not seem to affect him in any way.

The men in the jail were suffering from nerves. Somehow the word had gotten out that the vigilante organization was a reality, and that they were to be tried before a vigilante court. Joel Miller, hysterical, accused Middleton of double-crossing his men.

"Shut up, you fool!" snarled the sheriff, showing the strain under which he was laboring merely by the irascible edge on his voice. "Haven't you seen your friends drifting by the jail? I've gathered the men in from the hills. They're all here. Forty-odd men, every Vulture in the gang, is here in Whapeton.

"Now, get this: and McNab, listen closely: we'll stage the break just before daylight, when everybody is asleep. Just before dawn is the best time, because that's about the only time in the whole twenty-four hours that the camp isn't going full blast.

"Some of the boys, with masks on, will swoop down and overpower you deputies. There'll be no shots fired until they've gotten the prisoners and started off. Then start yelling and shooting after them--in the air, of course. That'll bring everybody on the run to hear how you were overpowered by a gang of masked riders.

"Miller, you and Letcher and Barlow will put up a fight--"

"Why?"

"Why, you fool, to make it look like it's a mob that's capturing you, instead of friends rescuing you. That'll explain why none of the deputies are hurt. Men wanting to lynch you wouldn't want to hurt the officers. You'll yell and scream blue murder, and the men in the masks will drag you out, tie you and throw you across horses and ride off. Somebody is bound to see them riding away. It'll look like a capture, not a rescue."

Bearded lips gaped in admiring grins at the strategy.

"All right. Don't make a botch of it. There'll be hell to pay, but I'll convince Hopkins that it was the work of a mob, and we'll search the hills to find your bodies hanging from trees. We won't find any bodies, naturally, but maybe we'll contrive to find a mass of ashes where a log hut had been burned to the ground, and a few hats and belt buckles easy to identify."

Miller shivered at the implication and stared at Middleton with painful intensity.

"Middleton, you ain't planning to have us put out of the way? These men in masks are our friends, not vigilantes you've put up to this?"

"Don't be a fool!" flared Middleton disgustedly. "Do you think the gang would stand for anything like that, even if I was imbecile enough to try it? You'll recognize your friends when they come.

"Miller, I want your name at the foot of a confession I've drawn up, implicating somebody as the leader of the Vultures. There's no use trying to deny you and the others are members of the gang. Hopkins knows you are; instead of trying to play innocent, you'll divert suspicion to someone outside the gang. I haven't filled in the name of the leader, but Dick Lennox is as good as anybody. He's a gambler, has few friends, and never would work with us. I'll write his name in your 'confession' as chief of the Vultures, and Corcoran will kill him 'for resisting arrest,' before he has time to prove that it's a lie. Then, before anybody has time to get suspicious, we'll make our last big haul--the raid on the Hopkins and Bisley cache!--and blow! Be ready to jump, when the gang swoops in.

"Miller, put your signature to this paper. Read it first if you want to. I'll fill in the blanks I left for the 'chief's' name later. Where's Corcoran?"

"I saw him in the Golden Eagle an hour ago," growled McNab. "He's drinkin' like a fish."

"Damnation!" Middleton's mask slipped a bit despite himself, then he regained his easy control. "Well, it doesn't matter. We won't need him tonight. Better for him not to be here when the jail break's made. Folks would think it was funny if he didn't kill somebody. I'll drop back later in the night."

Even a man of steel nerves feels the strain of waiting for a crisis. Corcoran was in this case no exception. Middleton's mind was so occupied in planning, scheming and conniving that he had little time for the strain to corrode his willpower. But Corcoran had nothing to occupy his attention until the moment came for the jump.

He began to drink, almost without realizing it. His veins seemed on fire, his external senses abnormally alert. Like most men of his breed he was high-strung, his nervous system poised on a hair-trigger balance, in spite of his mask of unemotional coolness. He lived on, and for, violent action. Action kept his mind from turning inward; it kept his brain clear and his hand steady; failing action, he fell back on whisky. Liquor artificially stimulated him to that pitch which his temperament required. It was not fear that made his nerves thrum so intolerably. It was the strain of waiting inertly, the realization of the stakes for which they played. Inaction maddened him. Thought of the gold cached in the cave behind John Middleton's cabin made Corcoran's lips dry, set a nerve to pounding maddeningly in his temples.

So he drank, and drank, and drank again, as the long day wore on.

The noise from the bar was a blurred medley in the back room of the Golden Garter. Glory Bland stared uneasily across the table at her companion. Corcoran's blue eyes seemed lit by dancing fires. Tiny beads of perspiration shone on his dark face. His tongue was not thick; he spoke lucidly and without exaggeration; he had not stumbled when he entered. Nevertheless he was drunk, though to what extent the girl did not guess.

"I never saw you this way before, Steve," she said reproachfully.

"I've never had a hand in a game like this before," he answered, the wild flame flickering bluely in his eyes. He reached across the table and caught her white wrist with an unconscious strength that made her wince. "Glory, I'm pullin' out of here tonight. I want you to go with me!"

"You're leaving Whapeton? *Tonight*?"

"Yes. For good. Go with me! This joint ain't fit for you. I don't know how you got into this game, and I don't give a damn. But you're different from these other dance hall girls. I'm takin' you with me. I'll make a queen out of you! I'll cover you with diamonds!"

She laughed nervously.

"You're drunker than I thought. I know you've been getting a big salary, but--"

"Salary?" His laugh of contempt startled her. "I'll throw my salary into the street for the beggars to fight over. Once I told that fool Hopkins that I had a gold mine right here in Whapeton. I told him no lie. I'm *rich*!"

"What do you mean?" She was slightly pale, frightened by his vehemence.

His fingers unconsciously tightened on her wrist and his eyes gleamed with the hard arrogance of possession and desire.

"You're mine, anyway," he muttered. "I'll kill any man that looks at you. But you're in love with me. I know it. Any fool could see it. I can trust you. You wouldn't dare betray me. I'll tell you. I wouldn't take you along without tellin' you the truth. Tonight Middleton and I are goin' over the mountains with a million dollars' worth of gold tied on pack mules!"

He did not see the growing light of incredulous horror in her eyes.

"A million in gold! It'd make a devil out of a saint! Middleton thinks he'll kill me when we get away safe, and grab the whole load. He's a fool. It'll be him that dies, when the time comes. I've planned while he planned. I didn't ever intend to split the loot with him. I wouldn't be a thief for less than a million."

"Middleton--" she choked.

"Yeah! He's chief of the Vultures, and I'm his right-hand man. If it hadn't been for me, the camp would have caught on long ago."

"But you upheld the law," she panted, as if clutching at straws. "You killed murderers--saved McBride from the mob."

"I killed men who tried to kill me. I shot as square with the camp as I could, without goin' against my own interests. That business of McBride has nothin' to do with it. I'd given him my word. That's all behind us now. Tonight, while the vigilantes and the Vultures kill each other, we'll *vamose*! And you'll go with me!"

With a cry of loathing she wrenched her hand away, and sprang up, her eyes blazing.

"Oh!" It was a cry of bitter disillusionment. "I thought you were straight--honest! I worshiped you because I thought you were honorable. So many men were dishonest and bestial--I idolized you! And you've just been pretending--playing a part! Betraying the people who trusted you!" The poignant anguish of her enlightenment choked her, then galvanized her with another possibility.

"I suppose you've been pretending with me, too!" she cried wildly. "If you haven't been straight with the camp, you couldn't have been straight with me, either! You've made a fool of me! Laughed at me and shamed me! And now you boast of it in my teeth!"

"Glory!" He was on his feet, groping for her, stunned and bewildered by her grief and rage. She sprang back from him.

"Don't touch me! Don't look at me! Oh, I hate the very sight of you!"

And turning, with an hysterical sob, she ran from the room. He stood swaying slightly, staring stupidly after her. Then fumbling with his hat, he stalked out, moving like an automaton. His thoughts were a confused maelstrom, whirling until he was giddy. All at once the liquor seethed madly in his brain, dulling his perceptions, even his recollections of what had just passed. He had drunk more than he realized.

Not long after dark had settled over Whapeton, a low call from the darkness brought Colonel Hopkins to the door of his cabin, gun in hand.

"Who is it?" he demanded suspiciously.

"It's Middleton. Let me in, quick!"

The sheriff entered, and Hopkins, shutting the door, stared at him in surprise. Middleton showed more agitation than the Colonel had ever seen him display. His face was pale and drawn. A great actor was lost to the world when John Middleton took the dark road of outlawry.

"Colonel, I don't know what to say. I've been a blind fool. I feel that the lives of murdered men are hung about my neck for all Eternity! All through my blindness and stupidity!"

"What do you mean, John?" ejaculated Colonel Hopkins.

"Colonel, Miller talked at last. He just finished telling me the whole dirty business. I have his confession, written as he dictated."

"He named the chief of the Vultures?" exclaimed Hopkins eagerly.

"He did!" answered Middleton grimly, producing a paper and unfolding it. Joel Miller's unmistakable signature sprawled at the bottom. "Here is the name of the leader, dictated by Miller to me!"

"Good God!" whispered Hopkins. "Bill McNab!"

"Yes! My deputy! The man I trusted next to Corcoran. What a fool--what a blind fool I've been. Even when his actions seemed peculiar, even when you voiced your suspicions of him, I could not bring myself to believe it. But it's all clear now. No wonder the gang always knew my plans as soon as I knew them myself! No wonder my deputies-- before Corcoran came--were never able to kill or capture any Vultures. No wonder, for instance, that Tom Deal 'escaped,' before we could question him. That bullet hole in McNab's arm, supposedly made by Deal--Miller told me McNab got that in a quarrel with one of his own gang. It came in handy to help pull the wool over my eyes.

"Colonel Hopkins, I'll turn in my resignation tomorrow. I recommend Corcoran as my successor. I shall be glad to serve as deputy under him."

"Nonsense, John!" Hopkins laid his hand sympathetically on Middleton's shoulder. "It's not your fault. You've played a man's part all the way through. Forget that talk about resigning. Whapeton doesn't need a new sheriff; you just need some new deputies. Just now we've got some planning to do. Where is McNab?"

"At the jail, guarding the prisoners. I couldn't remove him without exciting his suspicion. Of course he doesn't dream that Miller has talked. And I learned something else. They plan a jailbreak shortly after midnight."

"We might have expected that!"

"Yes. A band of masked men will approach the jail, pretend to overpower the guards--yes, Stark and Richardson are Vultures, too--and release the prisoners. Now this is my plan. Take fifty men and conceal them in the trees near the jail. You can plant some on one side, some on the other. Corcoran and I will be with you, of course. When the bandits come, we can kill or capture them all at one swoop. We have the advantage of knowing their plans, without their knowing we know them."

"That's a good plan, John!" warmly endorsed Hopkins. "You should have been a general. I'll gather the men at once. Of course, we must use the utmost secrecy."

"Of course. If we work it right, we'll bag prisoners, deputies and rescuers with one stroke. We'll break the back of the Vultures!"

"John, don't ever talk resignation to me again!" exclaimed Hopkins, grabbing his hat and buckling on his gun-belt. "A man like you ought to be in the Senate. Go get Corcoran. I'll gather my men and we'll be in our places before midnight. McNab and the others in the jail won't hear a sound."

"Good! Corcoran and I will join you before the Vultures reach the jail."

Leaving Hopkins' cabin, Middleton hurried to the bar of the King of Diamonds. As he drank, a rough-looking individual moved casually up beside him. Middleton bent his head over his whisky glass and spoke, hardly moving his lips. None could have heard him a yard away.

"I've just talked to Hopkins. The vigilantes are afraid of a jail break. They're going to take the prisoners out just before daylight and hang them out of hand. That talk about legal proceedings was just a bluff. Get all the boys, go to the jail and get the prisoners out within a half-hour after midnight. Wear your masks, but let there be no shooting or yelling. I'll tell McNab our plan's been changed. Go silently. Leave your horses at least a quarter of a mile down the gulch and sneak up to the jail on foot, so you won't make so much noise. Corcoran and I will be hiding in the brush to give you a hand in case anything goes wrong."

The other man had not looked toward Middleton; he did not look now. Emptying his glass, he strolled deliberately toward the door. No casual onlooker could have known that any words had passed between them.

When Glory Bland ran from the backroom of the Golden Garter, her soul was in an emotional turmoil that almost amounted to insanity. The shock of her brutal disillusionment vied with passionate shame of her own gullibility and an unreasoning anger. Out of this seething cauldron grew a blind desire to hurt the man who had unwittingly hurt her. Smarting vanity had its part, too, for with characteristic and illogical feminine conceit, she believed that he had practiced an elaborate deception in order to fool her into falling in love with him--or rather with the man she thought he was. If he was false with men, he must be false with women, too. That thought sent her into hysterical fury, blind to all except a desire for revenge. She was a primitive, elemental young animal, like most of her profession of that age and place; her emotions were powerful and easily stirred, her passions stormy. Love could change quickly to hate.

She reached an instant decision. She would find Hopkins and tell him everything Corcoran had told her! In that instant she desired nothing so much as the ruin of the man she had loved.

She ran down the crowded street, ignoring men who pawed at her and called after her. She hardly saw the people who stared after her. She supposed that Hopkins would be at the jail, helping guard the prisoners, and she directed her steps thither. As she ran up on the porch Bill McNab confronted her with a leer, and laid a hand on her arm, laughing when she jerked away.

"Come to see me, Glory? Or are you lookin' for Corcoran?"

She struck his hand away. His words, and the insinuating guffaws of his companions were sparks enough to touch off the explosives seething in her.

"You fool! You're being sold out, and don't know it!"

The leer vanished.

"What do you mean?" he snarled.

"I mean that your boss is fixing to skip out with all the gold you thieves have grabbed!" she blurted, heedless of consequences, in her emotional storm, indeed scarcely aware of what she was saying. "He and Corcoran are going to leave you holding the sack, tonight!"

And not seeing the man she was looking for, she eluded McNab's grasp, jumped down from the porch and darted away in the darkness.

The deputies stared at each other, and the prisoners, having heard everything, began to clamor to be turned out.

"Shut up!" snarled McNab. "She may be lyin'. Might have had a quarrel with Corcoran and took this fool way to get even with him. We can't afford to take no chances. We've got to be sure we know what we're doin' before we move either way. We can't afford to let you out now, on the chance that she might be lyin'. But we'll give you weapons to defend yourselves.

"Here, take these rifles and hide 'em under the bunks. Pete Daley, you stay here and keep folks shooed away from the jail till we get back. Richardson, you and Stark come with me! We'll have a showdown with Middleton right now!"

When Glory left the jail she headed for Hopkins' cabin. But she had not gone far when a reaction shook her. She was like one waking from a nightmare, or a dope-jag. She was still sickened by the discovery of Corcoran's duplicity in regard to the people of the camp, but she began to apply reason to her suspicions of his motives in regard to herself. She began to realize that she had acted illogically. If Corcoran's attitude toward her was not sincere, he certainly would not have asked her to leave the camp with him. At the expense of her vanity she was forced to admit that his attentions to her had not been necessary in his game of duping the camp. That was something apart; his own private business; it must be so. She had suspected him of trifling with her affections, but she had to admit that she had no proof that he had ever paid the slightest attention to any other woman in Whapeton. No; whatever his motives or actions in general, his feeling toward her must be sincere and real.

With a shock she remembered her present errand, her reckless words to McNab. Despair seized her, in which she realized that she loved Steve Corcoran in spite of all he might be. Chill fear seized her that McNab and his friends would kill her lover. Her unreasoning fury died out, gave way to frantic terror.

Turning she ran swiftly down the gulch toward Corcoran's cabin. She was hardly aware of it when she passed through the blazing heart of the camp. Lights and bearded faces were like a nightmarish blur, in which nothing was real but the icy terror in her heart.

She did not realize it when the clusters of cabins fell behind her. The patter of her slippered feet in the road terrified her, and the black shadows under the trees seemed pregnant with menace. Ahead of her she saw Corcoran's cabin at last, a light streaming through the open door. She burst into the office-room, panting--and was confronted by Middleton who wheeled with a gun in his hand.

"What the devil are you doing here?" He spoke without friendliness, though he returned the gun to its scabbard.

"Where's Corcoran?" she panted. Fear took hold of her as she faced the man she now knew was the monster behind the grisly crimes that had made a reign of terror over Whapeton Gulch. But fear for Corcoran overshadowed her own terror.

"I don't know. I looked for him through the bars a short time ago, and didn't find him. I'm expecting him here any minute. What do you want with him?"

"That's none of your business," she flared.

"It might be." He came toward her, and the mask had fallen from his dark, handsome face. It looked wolfish.

"You were a fool to come here. You pry into things that don't concern you. You know too much. You talk too much. Don't think I'm not wise to you! I know more about you than you suspect."

A chill fear froze her. Her heart seemed to be turning to ice. Middleton was like a stranger to her, a terrible stranger. The mask was off, and the evil spirit of the man was reflected in his dark, sinister face. His eyes burned her like actual coals.

"I didn't pry into secrets," she whispered with dry lips. "I didn't ask any questions. I never before suspected you were the chief of the Vultures--"

The expression of his face told her she had made an awful mistake.

"So you know that!" His voice was soft, almost a whisper, but murder stood stark and naked in his flaming eyes. "I didn't know that. I was talking about something else. Conchita told me it was you who told Corcoran about the plan to lynch McBride. I wouldn't have killed you for that, though it interfered with my plans. But you know too much. After tonight it wouldn't matter. But tonight's not over yet--"

"Oh!" she moaned, staring with dilated eyes as the big pistol slid from its scabbard in a dull gleam of blue steel. She could not move, she could not cry out. She could only cower dumbly until the crash of the shot knocked her to the floor.

As Middleton stood above her, the smoking gun in his hand, he heard a stirring in the room behind him. He quickly upset the long table, so it could hide the body of the girl, and turned, just as the door opened. Corcoran came from the back room, blinking, a gun in his hand. It was evident that he had just awakened from a drunken sleep, but his hands did not shake, his pantherish tread was sure as ever, and his eyes were neither dull nor bloodshot.

Nevertheless Middleton swore.

"Corcoran, are you crazy?"

"You shot?"

"I shot at a snake that crawled across the floor. You must have been mad, to soak up liquor today, of all days!"

"I'm all right," muttered Corcoran, shoving his gun back in its scabbard.

"Well, come on. I've got the mules in the clump of trees next to my cabin. Nobody will see us load them. Nobody will see us go. We'll go up the ravine beyond my cabin, as we planned. There's nobody watching my cabin tonight. All the Vultures are down in the camp, waiting for the signal to move. I'm hoping none will escape the vigilantes, and that most of the vigilantes themselves are killed in the fight that's sure to come. Come on! We've got thirty mules to load, and that job will take us from now until midnight, at least. We won't pull out until we hear the guns on the other side of the camp."

"Listen!"

It was footsteps, approaching the cabin almost at a run. Both men wheeled and stood motionless as McNab loomed in the door. He lurched into the room, followed by Richardson and Stark. Instantly the air was supercharged with suspicion, hate, tension. Silence held for a tick of time.

"You fools!" snarled Middleton. "What are you doing away from the jail?"

"We came to talk to you," said McNab. "We've heard that you and Corcoran planned to skip with the gold."

Never was Middleton's superb self-control more evident. Though the shock of that blunt thunderbolt must have been terrific, he showed no emotion that might not have been showed by any honest man, falsely accused.

"Are you utterly mad?" he ejaculated, not in a rage, but as if amazement had submerged whatever anger he might have felt at the charge.

McNab shifted his great bulk uneasily, not sure of his ground. Corcoran was not looking at him, but at Richardson, in whose cold eyes a lethal glitter was growing. More quickly than Middleton, Corcoran sensed the inevitable struggle in which this situation must culminate.

"I'm just sayin' what we heard. Maybe it's so, maybe it ain't. If it ain't, there's no harm done," said McNab slowly.

"On the chance that it was so, I sent word for the boys not to wait till midnight. They're goin' to the jail within the next half-hour and take Miller and the rest out."

Another breathless silence followed that statement. Middleton did not bother to reply. His eyes began to smolder. Without moving, he yet seemed to crouch, to gather himself for a spring. He had realized what Corcoran had already sensed; that this situation was not to be passed over by words, that a climax of violence was inevitable.

Richardson knew this; Stark seemed merely puzzled. McNab, if he had any thoughts, concealed the fact.

"Say you *was* intendin' to skip," he said, "this might be a good chance, while the boys was takin' Miller and them off up into the hills. I don't know. I ain't accusin' you. I'm just askin' you to clear yourself. You can do it easy. Just come back to the jail with us and help get the boys out."

Middleton's answer was what Richardson, instinctive man-killer, had sensed it would be. He whipped out a gun in a blur of speed. And even as it cleared leather, Richardson's gun was out. But Corcoran had not taken his eyes off the cold-eyed gunman, and his draw was the quicker by a lightning-flicker. Quick as was Middleton, both the other guns spoke before his, like a double detonation. Corcoran's slug blasted Richardson's brains just in time to spoil his shot at Middleton. But the bullet grazed Middleton so close that it caused him to miss McNab with his first shot.

McNab's gun was out and Stark was a split second behind him. Middleton's second shot and McNab's first crashed almost together, but already Corcoran's guns had sent lead ripping through the giant's flesh. His ball merely flicked Middleton's hair in passing, and the chief's slug smashed full into his brawny breast. Middleton fired again and yet again as the giant was falling. Stark was down, dying on the floor, having pulled trigger blindly as he fell, until the gun was empty.

Middleton stared wildly about him, through the floating blue fog of smoke that veiled the room. In that fleeting instant, as he glimpsed Corcoran's image-like face, he felt that only in such a setting as this did the Texan appear fitted. Like a somber figure of Fate he moved implacably against a background of blood and slaughter.

"God!" gasped Middleton. "That was the quickest, bloodiest fight I was ever in!" Even as he talked he was jamming cartridges into his empty gun chambers.

"We've got no time to lose now! I don't know how much McNab told the gang of his suspicions. He must not have told them much, or some of them would have come with him. Anyway, their first move will be to liberate the prisoners. I have an idea they'll go through with that just as we planned, even when McNab doesn't return to lead them. They won't come looking for him, or come after us, until they turn Miller and the others loose.

"It just means the fight will come within the half-hour instead of at midnight. The vigilantes will be there by that time. They're probably lying in ambush already. Come on! We've got to sling gold on those mules like devils. We may have to leave some of it; we'll know when the fight's started, by the sound of the guns! One thing, nobody will come up here to investigate the shooting. All attention is focused on the jail!"

Corcoran followed him out of the cabin, then turned back with a muttered: "Left a bottle of whisky in that back room."

"Well, hurry and get it and come on!" Middleton broke into a run toward his cabin, and Corcoran re-entered the smoke-veiled room. He did not glance at the crumpled bodies which lay on the crimson-stained floor, staring glassily up at him. With a stride he reached the back room, groped in his bunk until he found what he wanted, and then strode again toward the outer door, the bottle in his hand.

The sound of a low moan brought him whirling about, a gun in his left hand. Startled, he stared at the figures on the floor. He knew none of them had moaned; all three were past moaning. Yet his ears had not deceived him.

His narrowed eyes swept the cabin suspiciously, and focused on a thin trickle of crimson that stole from under the upset table as it lay on its side near the wall. None of the corpses lay near it.

He pulled aside the table and halted as if shot through the heart, his breath catching in a convulsive gasp. An instant later he was kneeling beside Glory Bland, cradling her golden head in his arm. His hand, as he brought the whisky bottle to her lips, shook queerly.

Her magnificent eyes lifted toward him, glazed with pain. But by some miracle the delirium faded, and she knew him in her last few moments of life.

"Who did this?" he choked. Her white throat was laced by a tiny trickle of crimson from her lips.

"Middleton--" she whispered. "Steve, oh, Steve--I tried--" And with the whisper uncompleted she went limp in his arms. Her golden head lolled back; she seemed like a child, a child just fallen asleep. Dazedly he eased her to the floor.

Corcoran's brain was clear of liquor as he left the cabin, but he staggered like a drunken man. The monstrous, incredible thing that had happened left him stunned, hardly able to credit his own senses. It had never occurred to him that Middleton would kill a woman, that any white man would. Corcoran lived by his own code, and it was wild and rough and hard, violent and incongruous, but it included the conviction that womankind was sacred, immune from the violence that attended the lives of men. This code was as much a vital, living element of the life of the Southwestern frontier as was personal honor, and the resentment of insult.

Without pompousness, without pretentiousness, without any of the tawdry glitter and sham of a false chivalry, the people of Corcoran's breed practiced this code in their daily lives. To Corcoran, as to his people, a woman's life and body were inviolate. It had never occurred to him that that code would, or could be violated, or that there could be any other kind.

Cold rage swept the daze from his mind and left him crammed to the brim with murder. His feelings toward Glory Bland had approached the normal love experienced by the average man as closely as was possible for one of his iron nature. But if she had been a stranger, or even a person he had disliked, he would have killed Middleton for outraging a code he had considered absolute.

He entered Middleton's cabin with the soft stride of a stalking panther. Middleton was bringing bulging buckskin sacks from the cave, heaping them on a table in the main room. He staggered with their weight. Already the table was almost covered.

"Get busy!" he exclaimed. Then he halted short, at the blaze in Corcoran's eyes. The fat sacks spilled from his arms, thudding on the floor.

"You killed Glory Bland!" It was almost a whisper from the Texan's livid lips.

"Yes." Middleton's voice was even. He did not ask how Corcoran knew, he did not seek to justify himself. He knew the time for argument was past. He did not think of his plans, or of the gold on the table, or that still back there in the cave. A man standing face to face with Eternity sees only the naked elements of life and death.

"Draw!" A catamount might have spat the challenge, eyes flaming, teeth flashing.

Middleton's hand was a streak to his gun butt. Even in that flash he knew he was beaten--heard Corcoran's gun roar just as he pulled trigger. He swayed back, falling, and in a blind gust of passion Corcoran emptied both guns into him as he crumpled.

For a long moment that seemed ticking into Eternity the killer stood over his victim, a somber, brooding figure that might have been carved from the iron night of the Fates. Off toward the other end of the camp other guns burst forth suddenly, in salvo after thundering salvo. The fight that was plotted to mask the flight of the Vulture chief had begun. But the figure which stood above the dead man in the lonely cabin did not seem to hear.

Corcoran looked down at his victim, vaguely finding it strange, after all, that all those bloody schemes and terrible ambitions should end like that, in a puddle of oozing blood on a cabin floor. He lifted his head to stare somberly at the bulging sacks on the table. Revulsion gagged him.

A sack had split, spilling a golden stream that glittered evilly in the candlelight. His eyes were no longer blinded by the yellow sheen. For the first time he saw the blood on that gold, it was black with blood; the blood of innocent men; the blood of a woman. The mere thought of touching it nauseated him, made him feel as if the slime that had covered John Middleton's soul would befoul him. Sickly he realized that some of Middleton's guilt was on his own head. He had not pulled the trigger that ripped a woman's life from her body; but he had worked hand-in-glove with the man destined to be her murderer--Corcoran shuddered and a clammy sweat broke out upon his flesh.

Down the gulch the firing had ceased, faint yells came to him, freighted with victory and triumph. Many men must be shouting at once, for the sound to carry so far. He knew what it portended; the Vultures had walked into the trap laid for them by the man they trusted as a leader. Since the firing had ceased, it meant the whole band were either dead or captives. Whapeton's reign of terror had ended.

But he must stir. There would be prisoners, eager to talk. Their speech would weave a noose about his neck.

He did not glance again at the gold, gleaming there where the honest people of Whapeton would find it. Striding from the cabin he swung on one of the horses that stood saddled and ready among the trees. The lights of the camp, the roar of the distant voices fell away behind him, and before him lay what wild destiny he could not guess. But the night was full of haunting shadows, and within him grew a strange pain, like a revelation; perhaps it was his soul, at last awakening.

THE END